HONOR BOUND

MILITARY ROMANCE — WITH A SCIENCE FICTION EDGE

ANN GIMPEL

Edited by
JENNIFER HASSANI
Illustrated by
FIONA JAYDE

CONTENTS

HONOR BOUND

GENTECH REBELLION, BOOK TWO

Military Romance
(with a science fiction edge)
By
Ann Gimpel

COPYRIGHT PAGE

***B*ook Description:**
Honor takes a huge chance and flees her compound one wintry night. A genetically altered woman, she has no memories from before her kin staged a rebellion seven years before. Because of her enhanced physiology, she finds a home working for the CIA alongside four other women just like her. There are still plenty of rules, but they're different, and she's figuring out how to blend in.

Milton Reins burns through women and marriages. After the third one implodes, he swears off hunting for a replacement. Running the CIA is a more than fulltime job. There's no time for anything else in his life, which is fine until Honor comes along. Training in the gym throws their bodies together and makes him remember the feel of a woman in his arms. Milton aches for her, but she's a freak—the CIA term for test tube humans designed by scientists.

Honor wants Milton with every bone in her body, but it's a terrible idea, especially after she delves into his head and sees his ambivalence toward her kind. Need drives them together, but their differences create roadblocks every step of the way. Fueled by anger and fear, she shuts him out. So what if the sex was great, she's done.

Or is she?

Series Backstory:

Sometime between the interminable wars in the Middle East and 9/11, the United States moved forward breeding a race of super humans. Clandestine labs formed, armed with eager scientists who'd always yearned to manipulate human DNA. At first the clones looked promising, growing to fighting size in as little as a dozen years, but V1 had design flaws.

Seven years ago, a rogue group turned on their creators, blew up the lab, and hit all the other breeding farms, freeing whomever they could find. In the intervening time, they've retreated to hidden compounds and created a society run by men. Women are kept on a tight leash because the men fear if they discover their innate power, they'd launch their own rebellion.

is it no less interesting as some real world events are pulled into the story, making it scarily plausible. What follows is an intense story that has elements of romance, adventure, intrigue and mystery. A really enjoyable read that sets up what I hope will be a pretty awesome series. TrishFLReader – Amazon Top 1000 reviewer

I absolutely loved the blend of science fiction and romance; I did not really expect that! I feel like a lot of books nowadays has only one note, especially when it comes to the science fiction genre. I haven't read a book that has successfully incorporated both elements in a while, so I was really excited to read this book. I was hooked immediately. CC2015 – Amazon Top 1000 Reviewer

*M*ilton Edward Reins III ducked and wove, staying one step ahead of the game—barely—while Honor and Charity, two genetically enhanced women, came at him from different directions. They were sparring in the workout arena located beneath the CIA compound in Langley, Virginia, a room as familiar as his office since he spent so much time there. He leaped, spun, and landed harder than he would've liked on the mat. At least he was still on his feet. Air whistled between his teeth. He grunted with effort and raised his arm to fend off Charity's forward drive.

He used her momentum to unbalance her enough to stumble. Once she was out of the action at least for a moment, he pivoted in time to meet Honor head on. She threw all her weight forward. When that didn't work, she jumped on him, and wound her long legs around his waist while she pummeled his shoulders and back with karate chops. The points of her breasts pushed into his chest, sending a different kind of sensation straight to his groin, but Milton redirected his thoughts and smirked. This kind of attack was easy to subvert. He jammed his hands between them and pushed hard on nerves that ran along the insides of both her legs. Her flesh felt wonderful beneath his fingers. Warm and pliant, with cords of muscle running beneath.

Can't think about that, either.

She yelped, and her legs loosened. Encouraged because he was winning, Milton levered her arms from around him, and she slid to the ground, dancing back out of his reach. Color splotched her face, and her chest heaved with each breath.

Damn, she looks amazing!

He wanted to pull her against him—up close and personal, but Charity rushed him. He barely twisted out of the way in time, using her momentum to drive her to the ground—again. He angled a leg and kicked gently, catching the side of her neck in a crucial spot with his foot. If they'd been in true combat, and he'd kicked harder, she'd have been dead. At least she would have been if she were a normal human. He wasn't certain if a blow to that particular nerve bundle would kill these gals.

Long, black hair bounced around Charity as she danced from foot to foot. She shoved it out of green eyes gleaming with enthusiasm. Her body was damn near perfect, just like all the genetically altered women. Though they looked much the same, with dark hair and those clear, emerald eyes, small differences made it possible to tell them apart.

Tall, with lithe, muscled grace, Charity bore down on him once more. She swaggered as if she had all the time in the world, but he wasn't fooled. She was catching her breath. Her body-hugging tights and sports bra under a thin T-shirt didn't leave much to the imagination. Neither did Honor's outfit. Like him, the women trained barefoot. He danced away from Charity's frontal attack, pivoting out of her reach. She made a face at him and cocked her head to one side, clearly considering what to do next.

Charity and Honor were breathing hard; small compensation, but it still pleased him. He'd taken a series of injections to make him more like the freaks—genetically modified humans who'd escaped the labs that spawned them seven years before and staged a rebellion—but it had proven a good investment. The MDs pitched a fit, told him he was too old to risk it, so he'd taken matters into his own hands. Setting up the IVs was a bitch, but he'd managed it. Good thing too, or he'd never have been able to hold his own in combat like this.

Honor twisted an arm around his shoulders, and he slithered out from under her iron grasp, feeling her push for entry into his mind. He slammed up a barrier to keep her out. He needed an edge, and having her intuit his next move by peeking would obliterate any advantage his years of mixed martial arts training conferred.

"Hey!" he protested. "You're cheating."

"Well…" Honor drew back and leaned her hands on her knees sucking air. "If we can't win any other way…"

"I'm with her." Charity draped an arm around her friend. She snorted and raked her hands through hair that had mostly escaped from her braids. "God almighty! I don't get why we can't win. There are two of us, for chrissakes. You may be the head of the CIA, but you're still only one dude."

Milton threw his head back and laughed. He'd more or less recovered during their brief break. The women came perilously close to *winning*, but he'd be damned if he'd tell them that. He glanced at the wall clock at the far end of the practice gym. "Lunch time." He clasped his hands together, pushing outward to stretch his back and shoulders. "You're due at the gun range afterward. I know you're not crazy about guns, but you need practice with them."

"So we'll see you tomorrow morning?" Honor asked.

"You got it, ladies." Milton grinned. "Same time, same station. If you're lucky, Glory, Faith, and Hope will wear me out this afternoon, and you'll have one up on me tomorrow."

"Fat fucking chance," Charity muttered.

Her profanity drew another laugh from Milton. "You've picked up bad habits pretty damned fast," he noted.

"Hell!" Honor rolled her eyes. "You should see her drink. The Nameless Ones never let us have liquor."

"They missed the boat on a lot of fronts," Milton said. "Now skedaddle, or you'll be late for weapons training."

The door at the far end of the gym swooshed open, and Roy Kincaid strolled in. "Hey, boss!" He snapped off a mock salute, probably to annoy Milton. Tall and rangy, his coppery hair was dyed black. As usual, it was too long, sweeping his collar. His blue eyes held a mischievous glint, and he wore faded jeans and a black turtleneck, topped by a plaid, flannel lumberman's jacket. It was still winter and colder than hell outside most of the time.

"You're such a pain in the ass, Kincaid," Milton snarled and drew a black long-sleeved T-shirt on over the silver tank top he'd been training in. Next he worked his legs into gray sweats.

"You don't really mean that," Honor chortled, and she and Charity loped the length of the spacious room to disappear out the door Roy entered through.

Milton sidled to a bar bolted to the wall. Once he got there, he tugged a towel off it and wiped sweat from his face and neck. The door shut behind the women, and he turned to Roy. "They're becoming strong fighters. Forcing them to not use their mental ability was an excellent idea."

"You didn't agree with me at first." Roy met him at the back of the gym. He pulled out a chair and dropped into it. "What made you change your mind?"

"They're women," Milton growled. "No matter what, I figured they'd never be a match for a man." He shook his head and pulled up a second chair, dropping the towel back over the bar before he sat. "Brother, was I ever wrong. Those gals are bitches on wheels."

"They are pretty amazing."

"Never thought I'd end up playing nursemaid to a group of Valkyries," Milton muttered.

Roy quirked a brow. "Is it all that bad?"

Milton adopted half a hangdog look and met Roy's direct blue gaze. "If you ever repeat this, Kincaid, I'll say you're delusional, but I'm enjoying the hell out of it. If the specter of war with those monstrosities wasn't hanging over our heads, I'd be happier than a pig rolling in garbage."

"What I don't get…" Roy narrowed his eyes, "…is how the women can be so awesome, and the genetically altered men such bastards. Nameless Ones my ass. Not only did they have names, but they kept the women under such tight control, I'm surprised they didn't slit the guys' throats while they slept."

"Mmph." Milton steepled his fingers together. "Remember all that data Glory downloaded from one of their computers when she merged with it?"

"How could I forget? Shit! She almost died doing that. I could live the rest of my life without a repeat of that level of drama."

"The genetic modifications had a different impact on the women than the men. They're stronger and much more adaptive—"

"Which is why the men kept them under such strict control," Roy finished for him. "Yeah, yeah, I know all that, but now that I've finally found someone to share my life, I want to take care of those fuckers once and for all."

"Dream on." Milton eyed him speculatively. "I'm glad you and Glory are so well-matched. What do you need? Why'd you hunt me down? Surely not to shoot the shit over current affairs."

Roy's expression turned serious. "I want you to come upstairs and take a look at the map we created. The one with Glory's information about the location of all the compounds like the one she and the other women came from."

"Say more." Milton crooked two fingers at Roy.

"Lights are going crazy all across the board. It appears the majority of the compounds are mobilizing. If there's a critical mass they need to accomplish anything, they have to be damned close to it."

"Crap! They're gearing up for something major."

"Unfortunately, it looks that way." Roy frowned. "I'd hoped we could hit a few more compounds and add more women to our special unit, but I doubt we'll have that kind of time."

"Maybe we will. There's a compound not far from here. We could be battle-ready by tonight. The women have trained for a few weeks. It's enough since we'll be with them, along with your team."

"Come look at the map first." Roy pushed to his feet. "Then we'll decide."

"We?"

Roy made a rude sound. "You, boss. I meant you." Another rude blat sounded. "It's actually a relief. I wouldn't take your job if they offered it to me trimmed in diamonds."

"Smart ass." Milton paced Roy the length of the arena and continued to walk next to him out the door and up the elevator to ground level.

"You're pretty quiet," Roy observed.

"How's Glory dealing with the destruction of her compound? Any guilt for playing an elemental part in leveling the only home she remembers?"

"It took a while, but she's okay with it now." Roy hesitated. "She's still sad the rest of the women in her dorm didn't trust her enough to come with her, but she's more than ready to co-opt other women into joining us in fighting the men. If there's one thing all the women have in common, it's their deep hatred for the Nameless Ones."

"Must be universal from compound to compound."

Roy stopped dead, considering Milton's statement. "I assumed it was, but in truth, I have no idea. Neither would the women since they were so isolated."

They stood near the middle of Langley's enormous campus in a sleeting rain under leaden skies, getting wetter by the moment. Milton grabbed Roy's arm and yanked. "We can debate that from inside." He broke into a run and headed for the building that housed his office and most of their computer systems, with Roy hard on his heels.

Milton skipped the elevator and pounded up four flights of stairs, shaking water off as he ran.

"It wouldn't kill you to take the elevator," Roy said from behind him.

"You're getting soft, Kincaid." Milton placed his palm on the scanner and opened the stairwell door that led to his suite of offices. Once he was in the hall, he turned to shoot a significant glance at his old friend. "Or maybe you just need more sleep."

"If you're inferring Glory and I entertain each other every night, you'd be absolutely right." Roy slugged him in the shoulder. "You should try it. When's the last time you got laid?"

Milton tried for a serious face, but couldn't pull it off. "That's not an appropriate question for your superior officer."

"Oh, so it's okay for you to mention my sex life, but not the other way around?"

"Stuff it, Kincaid." Milton pushed into the office beyond his where they'd set up the computer simulation of the compounds, and his good humor evaporated. He walked to the wall mounted map and stared at all the flaring lights in disbelief.

"Pretty sobering, huh?" Roy made his way to his side.

"When did this happen?" Milton pointed at the map. "I've been in the gym with the women since right after breakfast."

"Sometime between last night and this morning. Shit!" Roy tapped the display. "There's another one. That's number twenty. I counted before I came to find you."

Milton unclenched his jaw. "Do you suppose they figured out some way to mimic mobilization? They've likely guessed what Glory did, and their database brains would assume we've come up with a geographic simulation of their locations."

Roy creased his forehead into grim lines. "I have no fucking idea, but I like your explanation better than the other one."

"Which is they're gunning for us in real time. Probably not just us, either. Christ! I wonder what the collateral damage will be to civilians."

"Yeah." Roy's frown deepened. "It's what I'd do in their place. Strike fast and hard. It's been nearly a month since we blew up

Glory's compound. I've been expecting them to do something before now."

"I have too." Milton stripped off his wet top and went to a closet in the back of the room where he fetched a navy blue sweatshirt emblazoned with the CIA's logo. Shirt in hand, he pulled it over his head and walked back to the map, studying it.

"Look here." He ran his finger over a spot on the map. "This is the compound I'd thought to target next. It's close, just over the West Virginia line not far from Keyser."

"Well." Roy drew out the word. "At least it's not lit up like a fucking Christmas tree." He paused a beat. "Seems odd. They knew we annihilated Glory's compound, so they must've figured out where the women are. If that's true, it should be one of the first to mobilize."

"That'd be logical." Milton slapped his hand on a nearby table. "Adds credibility to my theory that maybe they're fucking with us by creating the illusion they're sending thousands of super humans on the warpath."

Roy turned to face his boss. "It's your call. What do you want to do?"

"I have a few competing ideas I need to work through. Call your team in for a briefing at thirteen hundred hours."

"What about Honor and Charity? Aren't they due at the munitions range then?"

Milton turned it over in his mind. "Maybe we just want your core team at first. In case there are some hard decisions to make."

Emotion played over Roy's face, but he didn't say anything.

"Spit out whatever it is." Milton made come along motions with two fingers.

Roy squared his shoulders. "The women see themselves as your team. You set things up that way to get Glory out from under a direct line of command to me. They're not going to like it if you don't include them in something big like this."

"I'll take it under advisement. Was there anything else?"

Roy smirked. "You never did like having your decisions questioned. Nope. I'm out of here. If you need me, I'll be in my office. And I'll muster my part of the troops for that thirteen hundred meeting."

Milton watched the door shut behind Roy before he perched on the edge of a chair and studied the map some more. At least no new lights started blinking. What did it mean? Were the men in those locations truly getting ready to move against them? What did they have in mind? Mental warfare? Chemical assaults? Or something more prosaic—like bombs?

He scrubbed the heels of his hands down his face, wishing to hell he had better intel. Or that some of the biochemists and genetic engineers who'd developed the mutant humans were available. They were among the first killed when the freaks, sick to death of being experimental targets, rebelled against their masters and escaped the breeding farms to set up their own compounds. In the intervening time, they'd engaged in small scale guerilla warfare against the government, but nothing major.

Apparently, that was all about to change.

After a last look at the map, he made his way out the door and down the hallway to his office, where he got a sandwich out of the refrigerator. He ate standing up, looking out the window at the Langley campus. He'd headed up the CIA for the last fifteen years. Compared with his early years in Vietnam's steamy jungles, this life was easy. Or it had been. At least in Vietnam, he'd been a solo operative. If he fucked up, the only one who bought it was him.

If he guessed wrong about what the freaks were up to now, tens of thousands of innocent people could die. A glance at the clock told him he had half an hour before meeting with Roy and his men. What about the women? Should he include them?

Milton shut his eyes. The vision that formed behind his lids was Honor wrapped around his body, her heat and her decidedly female scent surrounding him right along with her legs. Roy's flip question about when he'd been laid last rose to taunt him. He hadn't had sex in months—maybe as much as a year. When you cut to the chase, he was married to the CIA, and she was a jealous mistress. No other woman had been able to stand up to the demands work placed on him, and after three failed marriages, he'd decided it was better not to go that route again.

Thank fucking God he'd never had any kids. Especially sons. They'd have idolized him, wanted to follow his footsteps into danger, and there would've been one more domestic blowup just waiting to slap him in the face. He understood women. They guarded their offspring with the energy and single-mindedness of a lioness protecting her kill. If anything happened to the sons he'd never had because they were adrenaline junkies like him, he'd never have heard the end of it.

He forced his eyes open, pushed himself to focus. The last thing he needed right now was a trip into the emotional side he kept tightly shuttered. No wives. No kids. He aimed to keep it that way.

Milton took a bite of air and realized he'd finished his sandwich. He turned away from the window and paced from one end of his roomy office to the other as he thought about their next move. Too bad he couldn't find one of the male freaks and convince him to become a double agent. That scenario would provide a ready source of the intel he lacked.

Another glance at the clock told him he had five minutes. Maybe what Roy said about the women being furious if he left them out was right on. If anyone would know, he would, since he and Glory were married all but for the ceremony. Maybe there was something they'd missed in all the data Glory downloaded from the computer in her compound just before Roy blew the place to kingdom come.

Maybe I just want to see Honor again—before tomorrow morning's practice session.

The thought brought him up short, and he gave himself a sharp mental slap. When he started putting his needs above those of The Company—never mind the American public—it was time to either rearrange his priorities or move on.

He was out of time. Not quite trusting his motives, he picked up the smart phone on his desk and tapped it. When he heard the cheery voice asking what he wanted, he replied, "Call the gun range."

"Calling gun range," the phone app shot back.

Milton smiled. Wouldn't it be spiffy if his men—and women—responded with the same alacrity?

When the arms master answered, he instructed him to send the women back to the meeting room down the hall from his office.

CHAPTER 2

"I'll race you!" Charity shouted over her shoulder once she and Honor cleared the building with the underground practice gym.

They had plenty of time to make the gun range, so they didn't have to run anywhere, but Charity threw down the gauntlet, and Honor couldn't resist her challenge.

"Not fair," Honor yelled. "You're twenty feet ahead." But the other woman had already lit her afterburners and dashed across Langley's grounds using her enhanced physiology. With a screech that would've done a banshee proud, Honor sprinted after her, splashing through puddles and enjoying the cold rain pelting down. It was a good contrast to other parts of her that were much too warm. Water sprayed her face and dripped down her overheated body.

It felt good to go all out. To actually use the physical prowess built into her musculature. She was faster and stronger than any human—male or female—which was why she didn't understand how Milton kept beating them. Sure, he'd had the injections, but they didn't confer all the advantages of her petri dish birth and development. She thought about when she all but threw herself into his arms, wrapping herself around him as she tried to knock him to the ground. He hadn't even blinked, and the touch of his fingers on her inner thighs had been electric. Until he'd pressed on some nerves that hurt like hell...

To erase Milton from her mind, she put everything she had into catching Charity, but the woman held onto her lead. Finally, after a half dozen circuits through jogging trails weaving across the campus, Honor got close enough to grab her shoulder. "Got ya!" she panted.

"Only because I let you," Charity retorted, but she did slow down.

The women fell into an easy lope and made their way to the building where they lived. Honor's hair was plastered against her head from the rain, and she realized she should've worn a jacket and long pants, since she was wet clear through to her skin. "Gotta change before gun practice," she said and skittered through the door Charity opened.

"No kidding." Charity stopped in the lobby of their building. Water puddled around her feet, dripping off her hair and clothing. "At least we have better clothes than they gave us in the compound." She plucked at the sweatshirt she'd tossed over her workout duds.

Honor made a dismissive grunt. "Anything would be better." She thinned her lips into a harsh line. "Now that I know a little bit about how things work, in addition to all their other sins, the Nameless Ones were cheap sons of bitches. They did the bare minimum they could for us—and still keep us alive."

"They saw us as expendable." Charity nodded at the guard and pushed into a stairwell heading up to their third floor apartments.

"It was also another way to control us," Honor said thoughtfully. "We were dependent on them for everything: food, clothes, heat, even exercise. When they tossed us in those iso cells, we didn't see outside for weeks on end."

"Yeah." Charity pulled a sour face. "Prisoners of war have more rights than we did." She shook her head. "That's over with. I wasn't sure when we first got here, but I'm finally starting to feel safe. At least a little bit."

"Me too." Honor stopped in front of Charity's apartment. Hers was the next one down. "See you in a few? We can catch lunch in the cafeteria before we head for target practice."

The other woman narrowed her green eyes. "How about if you grab your clothes and come on back here? Or I could do the same. I want to talk with you."

"And you don't want anyone to overhear us?" At Charity's nod, Honor went on, "We could use telepathy."

"We could," Charity agreed, "but we have these few minutes while we're changing. Why waste power if we don't have to."

"Good point. Back in a flash."

Honor strode briskly to her door. When she got there, she tilted her chin, so the retinal scanner could read her eye and unlock the door. As she gathered dry clothes and a stout pair of boots, she thought about what Charity said. Everything they did that burned up electrical brain impulses meant they needed a bit of recovery time. If the task was small—like telepathic speech, for instance—the energy debit was barely noticeable. Something like Glory did when she tapped into the compound computer the night she rescued them and downloaded every scrap of data in sight would've been a real power hog.

With a final glance around to make certain she didn't forget anything she'd need, Honor made her way back down the hall and tapped on Charity's door. It sprang open immediately.

The other woman tossed a towel her way. "Your hair's dripping."

"No shit." Honor toed off her sodden running shoes and hastily stripped to her skin, hanging her wet clothes over chair backs in the small kitchen. She dried herself and started to get into the clothes she brought from her apartment. Charity, already dressed, sat in a chair watching her.

"What did you want to talk about?" Honor asked and wound the towel around her hair. "I may as well have changed in my own room for all the information you've shared since I got here."

"You like him, don't you?" Charity blurted and cast an appraising glance at Honor.

"Huh? Who?"

Charity rolled her eyes. "Milton. You were falling all over him today—and it's not the first time."

Honor clacked her jaws shut and pulled the towel off her hair, draping it over a nearby table. "Your point?"

"Look." Charity never took her unwavering gaze off Honor. "I know it worked out for Glory with Roy, but I, um, took a peek into Milton's past."

"You did what?" Honor rounded on her. "You could've gotten all of us kicked out of here."

A feral smile split Charity's face. "Not much chance of that. I know how to cover my tracks. How the hell do you think I found out all the stuff I did back at the compound?"

Honor had never really thought about it. *Back at the compound* didn't matter, but this did. "What'd you do?" She pulled on underwear, black trousers, and a thick pair of socks. Retrieving her boots, she pushed into them, doing up the laces as she listened.

"I hacked into the CIA personnel database." Pride underscored Charity's words. "But I did it because I was trying to protect you." She got to her feet and placed her hands on her hips. "Do you want to know what I found?"

"It couldn't be very bad, or they wouldn't let Milton run the CIA." Honor felt her stomach twist into an uncomfortable knot. Whatever her friend uncovered must be serious, or Charity wouldn't have gone to so much trouble to make sure she knew about it.

"If you don't want to know, I'll keep it to myself." Charity sounded hurt when she dropped her arms to her sides. She trotted across the room and pulled a jacket off a hook by the door. "We can leave. I thought you'd be grateful. Just because we're free women, it..." Her voice trailed off. "What I meant to say is freedom cuts both ways. We're free to make mistakes now—mistakes we never even considered when we lived in the compound."

Honor exhaled sharply and slid a black long-sleeved stretchy shirt and sweater on. Even though she could wear colors now, she was still more comfortable in black and gray. Part of her didn't want to hear whatever Charity had unearthed, but... "Tell me, already. With a lead-in like that, curiosity will eat me alive."

"You do like him, huh? I'm right about that?"

Honor shut her eyes for a moment. "Yes," she sputtered through clenched teeth. "I like him. It's not a crime. He's damned attractive with that salt and pepper hair and those bottomless dark eyes. Crap! His muscles are amazing in that tank top he wears when we spar. They flex when he moves, and—" She bit back a flood of longing, along with her words. "Never mind," she muttered, feeing like an ass.

Charity nodded sagely. "I knew it." She pounded a fist into her open palm. "Sweetie, he's been married like three times."

"So?"

"He's obviously a womanizer." Charity tilted her chin. "I've watched movies about men like him. If he were able to be faithful, he'd still be with wife number one."

Honor gestured with one hand. "What else did you dig up?"

"Isn't that enough?"

Honor thought about it. When she spoke, her words came slowly. "I truly appreciate that you're watching out for me—"

"We have to keep an eye on one another," Charity broke in. "Sure, it's not the compound, but still... They're regular humans, and we're something different. Their goodwill toward us could evaporate like yesterday's news, especially if the Nameless Ones retaliate for Roy blowing up our compound."

Honor drew her brows together. "I'll get back to Milton in a minute. What you just said about the Nameless Ones. Don't you think they'd have done something by now if they were going to?"

The other woman shook her head. "I have no fucking idea. Hope and I have turned it around and around, but we just don't know enough about how the Nameless Ones think. They obviously had a plan when they planted those spies here at Langley."

"Yeah, they were going to drag Glory back to the compound. Thank God she figured out something wasn't right, and Roy killed that one dude before he could hurt her. Milton ferreted out who the rest of the spies were. They're all in iso cells."

"Which is another reason I assumed the rest of them would stage something drastic to free those six guys." Charity pointed to a wall clock. "We only have a couple minutes."

Honor slipped her arms into her jacket. "Frankly, I'm more worried about whatever the Nameless Ones have up their sleeve than I am about Milton. We don't know what happened to his marriages. When you get down to it, we don't know very much about normal humans. How they interact with each other. What's important to them. What isn't. The only thing we know about love and marriage is what we've seen on television and in movies or picked up off the Internet. It might be a long way from how things really are."

"You're making excuses for him," Charity sputtered. "Maybe, if he'd only had one marriage crash and burn. But three? I tell you, he must have some really horrible habits. My first guess is he's a player." She stopped to take a breath. "I've seen how he looks at you out of the corners of his eyes, but only when he thinks your attention is elsewhere."

"Really?" Honor's heart gave an odd little flutter.

"Fuck!" Charity screwed her face into a disgusted moue and headed for the door. "I shouldn't have told you that. It's like throwing fat on a fire. How about if you just screw him and get it over with, and then—"

"Stop! Just stop!" Honor's voice was sharper than she'd meant it to be, but she didn't apologize. "The Nameless Ones planned my life right down to when I took a crap for seven years. I'm sure someone else controlled my every move during the years before that, but none of us have any memories of before the rebellion. No matter how well intentioned you are, I will not have you start doing the same thing."

"Point taken. Shall we?" Charity yanked the door open. Her mouth was set in angry lines, and her spine ramrod straight.

"I know your intentions were good—" Honor began as she tried to smooth the waters.

Charity made a chopping motion with one hand and walked out into the corridor. "It doesn't matter. If I find out anything else, I'll let you know—whether you want me to or not." She glanced over her shoulder. "Pull the door hard. The latch is finicky."

"What we need to do…" Honor followed her friend into the stairwell and down the steps, "is set our minds to create some probability models of what the Nameless Ones will do next. We did a little bit when we first got here, but never got as far as where they'll strike. Who they'll target. I've just assumed it would be here, but maybe they'll do something much more dramatic."

"Like blow up some big urban area to get everyone's attention? And then let the media know that if the CIA returns us to our rightful place with the Nameless Ones, the carnage will vanish?"

Honor's eyes widened. "Crap. No wonder you said what you did earlier about being careful. You don't trust the normal humans' kindness toward us." Honor nodded at the guard and pushed the front door to their building open. At least it had stopped raining, but the skies were still gunmetal colored.

"Hell no, I don't trust it," Charity murmured, keeping her voice low. "Why should I?" She placed her mouth close to Honor's ear. "Roy loves Glory. That's clear enough, but the CIA would never have offered us a home if they didn't want something from us."

"So what? Everybody always wants something. They want us to fight on their side with our augmented brains and bodies."

"I think they were hoping we'd know more about the men. After all, it's the Nameless Ones who've set traps and killed Roy's agents all these years he's been hunting them."

Honor stopped shy of the side door into the cafeteria. Charity's blatant dissection of them still being expendable—cannon fodder in the war between her kind and non-augmented humans—hadn't occurred to her. "You said you and Hope have talked. Has Faith been in on those discussions?"

Charity shook her head. "No. She and Glory are close, and we were worried our fears would find their way to Roy." Her eyes glittered defiantly. "What saved us from punishment at the hands of the Nameless Ones was keeping quiet about almost everything."

Honor's stomach twisted into a sour lump and hunger fled. "Sometimes," she said very quietly, "we're able to create reality with our thoughts. If I were you, I'd jettison all that negativity."

"So we're caught unaware when our captors throw us to the wolves?"

Honor glanced around and switched to telepathic speech, worried someone would overhear and brand them traitors. That could get them *thrown to the wolves* faster than damn near anything.

"In the first place, we're not prisoners," she said.

"The hell we're not." Charity didn't bother with telepathy. "Have any of us left here?"

"Glory has."

Charity grunted dismissively. "Yeah, with Roy. That scarcely counts."

Honor dropped her hands onto the other woman's shoulders and stared at her. "That first morning when we all gathered in that big meeting room, Milton and Roy gave us a choice. They said we didn't have to do anything. That fighting on their side was an option."

Another snort. "We should've tested their offer. None of us did, and now we're stuck here until the Nameless Ones up the ante so much we end up sacrificial sheep."

Honor tightened her fingers on Charity's shoulders. She wanted to shake sense into the other woman. Instead, she forced herself to let go. "You've spent too much time watching B grade movies. I'm not hungry. I'll see you at the gun range. Try not to shoot anyone by accident."

"If I wanted to kill someone," Charity's voice followed Honor as she hurried in the other direction, "I don't need guns or bullets, and neither do you."

Honor settled into a lope. The indoor gun range was over a mile away. She'd get there early, but the chill air gave her a chance to think. At least the rain had slowed to a drizzle. How could she have possibly missed such dramatic polarization among the five of them? Charity and Hope had breathed life into conspiracy theories, making them real.

Honor engaged her central processing unit brain and reviewed every single word, action, and suggestion from Roy, Milton, and the men on Roy's team since the night she'd met them at her compound. She hunted for double meanings, any indication she and the women were pawns in some master game.

She came up with a few questionable incidents, but they'd seemed like teasing at the time, a sport she and the girls weren't at all familiar with. She'd worked at recognizing humor during her time with the humans but found it challenging. Honor clamped her jaws together. No matter how she arranged the game pieces, she wasn't able to see the threats that had Charity and Hope so spun out.

Maybe it's like Milton and his three wives. Charity could be misinterpreting that too.

The outline of the building where she and the others learned how to handle weaponry came into view. Glory sprinted out a side door followed by Hope and Faith.

"Hiya!" Glory scooped Honor into a quick hug.

Despite herself, Honor grinned at Glory. If it weren't for her courage, she, Faith, Hope, and Charity would've died. They'd believed Glory when she rousted them out of their beds that night and told them they had to come with her—that she was offering them an opportunity to escape the Nameless Ones. If they'd given in to their doubts, like the seven other women in their dorm, they'd have blown sky high along with the rest of their compound. Honor closed her teeth over her lower lip not liking the direction of her thoughts.

"Something wrong?" Glory quirked a brow.

"Yes, but I don't want to talk about it right now. How was target practice?"

"Fine. We ended late, and we're heading back to the main building for a quick bite. A to-go bite, actually. There's some special meeting. You'll hear about it from the arms master since your afternoon practice got canceled."

Trepidation sent icy tentacles skidding down Honor's spine. Changes in plans rarely presaged anything good. "What kind of meeting?"

"Not sure. About all I know is that it's with Roy's team and Milton. The Nameless Ones are mobilizing—or it appears they are from what Milton told the arms master who told us to show up for the meeting—and we have to decide what to do."

Tension flowed from Honor as she blew out a lungful of air. "In lots of ways that's a relief," she muttered.

"Isn't it?" Hope and Faith closed from behind her, speaking almost in unison.

Faith laughed. "I've lost more than a few nights' sleep wondering when those bastards would show themselves. At least now we have something we can fight."

"Maybe," Glory cautioned. "Roy said it was possible the Nameless Ones are jimmying our electronic map somehow."

"If we're walking back, we need to get moving," Honor said. "No reason for us to check in with the arms master if he's just going to tell us what we already know." She didn't care for her thoughts as she eyed Hope, Charity's co-conspirator. Maybe the two of them had culled through the CIA's computers and found something Charity hadn't told her—something to fuel their sedition theories.

Stop it! Pretty soon, I'll be seeing boogeymen behind every bush.

She set a quick pace, gratified when the other women fell in next to and behind her. When had trust among them become so fragile? The answer came fast, arrowing straight into her guts.

When we had the Nameless Ones as a common enemy, things were much clearer.

Was that happening? Were Charity and Hope unconsciously recreating an emotional comfort zone where it was them against the world? The more Honor thought about it, the likelier it seemed. She considered having a private conversation with Glory and Faith but discarded the idea immediately. Working alone was what got Charity and Hope so panicked out.

No, if they were going to talk, it had to be all of them, and sooner rather than later.

CHAPTER 3

*M*ilton stood at the head of the large, windowless meeting room and watched everyone file in. Roy and his team of five men sat along one side of the long wooden table. There were originally six on Roy's team, but one had been a Nameless One who'd infiltrated their ranks so easily it still rankled. The women sat along the other side of the table. Milton's gaze lingered over Honor, but he dragged his attention away. The last thing he needed was an emotional entanglement.

Yeah, just keep telling myself that...

He clicked a few buttons, and a simulation of the map he'd studied earlier flickered to life on a huge screen at the far end of the room. A point of light represented each compound the genetically altered humans built for themselves after the rebellion. Some of those points held a red cast, which meant an unusual amount of activity noted by satellite surveillance.

Charlie McClaren whistled long and low, staring at the map through narrowed brown eyes. Like all of Roy's team, he dyed his hair jet black. A pair of green camouflage jeans covered his legs, and he wore a black T-shirt with the CIA logo blazoned across the back. "When did all that happen?" He pointed at the display.

"Sometime between midnight and now." Milton glanced around at the group.

Roy cleared his throat. "Did you decide how you'd like to proceed, sir?"

"Not exactly." Milton strode to a white board hung on a side wall and pointed to what he'd sketched on it earlier. "The way I see it, we have three choices." He held up a finger. "One. We wait until they attack and design defensive maneuvers once it happens. That'd probably the safest approach."

Milton raised a second finger. "Two. We target each compound that's lit up on the map and send jet fighters to bomb the living shit out of them. It's a tad on the Draconian side, but—"

"If you do that, you'll dump the U.S. right into World War III, and it'll kill bunches of civilians," Roy muttered. "Plus they'll fight back to the last freak, er man." He sent a glance skittering Glory's way.

None of the women liked it when anyone referred to the genetically altered humans as freaks, but it was a hard habit to break. Milton said, "Sorry, ladies. Moving on to our third option." He pressed his mouth into a thoughtful line. "This one is even riskier than door number two, but hear me out. I'm thinking it's unlikely the freaks—" He rolled his eyes. "Sorry again. We need to coin another term, but that's a low priority. What's important is that I'm not certain the compounds have mobilized to the extent the map indicates."

"How could the satellites lie?" Glory asked.

Milton wasn't used to anyone asking questions before he solicited them, but the women didn't operate by the same rules as his hand-picked cadre of CIA operatives. "It's not that the satellites are lying. But the freaks, er people, living in the compounds could simulate a high level of activity because they suspect we've mapped their locations and are watching them."

Milton hurried on before anyone else interrupted. "If that's the case, door number three is business as usual, except I want to speed up our timeline and hit the closest compound tonight. Maybe we'll gather more women to join us."

"Perhaps even some men," Charlie broke in. "I can't believe all of them want to commit suicide by throwing their lives away on a lost cause."

Milton stared at him and said, "Hold your comments until I ask for them."

"But Glory just asked a question," Charlie protested. "Why can't—?"

Roy elbowed him in the ribs, and Charlie retreated into a sullen silence.

"Better." Milton let his gaze settle briefly on everyone in the room. "This isn't exactly a democratic process because the final call is mine. The flak is too if I fuck up and guess wrong. Recapping. We have a choice of full offense, full defense, or business as usual with an accelerated timeline." He picked up a marker and faced the white board, drawing three columns, which he subdivided into two smaller columns each. "All right, people. Pros and cons for each alternative."

"Full offense is overkill," Roy stated flatly. "You put out the call about three weeks ago for amnesty. Have you gotten any takers?"

Milton shook his head. "Not a one."

"Are you certain the compounds got the message?" Faith asked.

"I don't see why they wouldn't have," Milton countered. "We hit every Internet venue, plus the major news outlets for television."

Glory raised her hand.

"You don't have to do that," Milton said. "Tell us what you're thinking."

Glory twisted so she could see the women lined up on her side of the table. "It's possible the compound leaders could've blocked that particular item from the feed." She touched Honor's arm. "What do you think? You worked more closely with communications than I did."

Honor's forehead creased into worried lines. "It's possible."

"More than possible," Faith cut in. "Likely. The Nameless Ones controlled us by making sure we were only exposed to what they wanted us to know. Why wouldn't they apply the same standards to the men?"

"Charity. Hope." Glory tilted her chin their way. "Ideas?"

"I agree with Faith," Hope said. "This compound that's close. How big is it?"

"They're all about the same size from what we can tell," Roy said. "The buildings and layout were cut from common plans. Why?"

"Their map location isn't lit, right?" she persisted without answering Roy.

"That's right." Roy left his seat and made his way to the map on the wall where he tapped the West Virginia location.

"Since the half dozen locations closest to it are lit up," Hope said thoughtfully, "maybe it means that particular compound refused to go along with the program."

Honor clapped her hands together. "Brilliant, Hope!" Her smile faded. "Not that it means they'll welcome us with open arms, but maybe we'll get a sizeable number of recruits if we hit their location."

"Or maybe it's a trap," Charity cut in. "They know they're closest to us. They could be trying to lure us to where they can do maximum damage."

Roy caught Glory's attention. "Run the odds," he said, his voice tinged with grim determination. "I will too. Let's see if we come up with the same answer."

"Do you want us to do it too?" Charity asked with an edge in her voice Milton couldn't interpret.

Roy turned to face her. "No. You already have a negative predisposition. Honor and Hope have a positive one. I'm hoping for a neutral assessment."

Charity surged to her feet, fists balled at her sides. "But our minds don't work like that. We're immune from emotional fallout—"

"Stop right there." Steel in Roy's voice cut off her words. "Our job as a group is to advise Milton to the best of our ability. What that means is we keep whatever personal agendas we might have out of the picture. Understood?"

Charity sat back down, but the surly expression on her face gave Milton pause. Clearly she wasn't happy about standing down when she had divergent opinions, although she must've done plenty of that in her compound. He hoped their decision to use the women wouldn't come back to bite him in the ass. Glory had been cooperative, but these other four hadn't been battle tested—yet.

"The odds…" Glory's clear voice rammed into his thoughts, "are seventy-five point two percent that the West Virginia compound defied some central command and twenty-four point eight percent that they're setting a trap for us."

"My numbers aren't quite that good," Roy said. "Sixty-eight versus thirty-two."

"How about something like this?" Charlie spoke up. "We hit the compound, but ask the Air Force for aerial backup—in case the lack of mobilization is a decoy."

"Keep the ideas coming." Milton spread his arms wide. "Once I've heard enough, I'll let you know."

HONOR CAST a surreptitious glance at the clock mounted near the ceiling at the far end of the room. It was almost six o'clock, and they'd been batting ideas around for so long she felt numb. Her stomach cramped, and she regretted her decision to skip lunch.

"I have enough." Milton's rumbling bass chopped into the fog her brain had turned into. "All of you can hit the cafeteria. Grab something to eat and meet me back here at nineteen hundred for your orders."

A chorus of, "Yes, sirs," echoed around the room, and chairs scraped noisily against the cream-colored linoleum floor as everyone got up to leave.

Honor got to her feet and rolled her shoulder blades to get some feeling back into her body. She wasn't used to sitting for such long periods of time. Glory punched her in the arm as she walked by and followed Roy out the door.

"Coming?" Charity asked.

"Yeah." Honor made her way to the door, still feeling rummy. Maybe food would help.

"Want to grab sandwiches and eat in one of our rooms?" Hope asked. "The cafeteria's pretty noisy."

And not very private.

Hope's voice was carefully neutral, but Honor understood her well enough. Maybe they did need to talk, but Glory needed to be a part of things. Except she was long gone.

Honor kept her thoughts to herself, even after they were settled in a circle on the floor of Charity's apartment. She inhaled half her roast beef sandwich without tasting it—eating for sustenance, not enjoyment—and washed it down with orange flavored mineral water. Conversation rose and fell around her, but no one said anything important, almost as if they didn't want to kick that particular door open—the one that might blow her earlier argument with Charity into a full-fledged confrontation.

After the last of her sandwich was gone, Honor raised her gaze to the other women and dove in headfirst. "Hope wanted us here so we could talk. What did you think about this afternoon's meeting?"

"Well, we almost weren't part of it," Hope said.

"How could you possibly know that?" Honor asked.

"I looked into Roy's head. Milton didn't want us there, but Roy said we had to be. Guess he won."

Honor shook her head. "Why wouldn't he want us to be a part of something that concerns our kin? Never mind there's no love lost between us and the Nameless Ones. Still, they're the closest thing to family that we have."

"That's why." Charity stabbed the air with her index finger. "He's afraid we won't be rational. That we'll go all soft and gushy and female on him." Anger flashed from her green eyes. "They underestimate us. Just like the Nameless Ones did. If we end up going to that compound, I say we develop our own plan—and put it into action after we get there."

"That's what Glory did," Hope chimed in.

"Yes, but she had a good reason," Faith said. "We can't go off fighting our own war."

"Why not?" Charity demanded. "We're smarter than them. I still think the reason that compound's gone dark is to lure us into making a mistake."

"In the first place," Honor put in, "they haven't *gone dark*. They just don't seem to be the hotbed of activity the other compounds are. In the second, I don't think it's a good idea to go off half-cocked with our own agenda."

"Maybe Milton and them are the ones going off half-cocked," Hope countered. "We're used to working as a team."

"So are they," Honor said. "Where would Glory fit into all this?"

Charity shrugged. "She threw in her lot with Roy, so I guess she'd be on their side."

Alarms went off deep inside Honor, and she scrambled to her feet. "If there are *sides*, Charity, it's the Nameless Ones on one of them, and us and our allies on the other."

"I haven't forgotten," the other woman said hotly.

"Did I miss something?" Faith looked confused. "When did we end up at each other's throats?"

"Excellent question," Honor gritted out. She let her gaze settle on her three friends in turn. "Glory went off on her own and almost ended up dead. If Roy hadn't been quick on his mental feet, she would've died in that tunnel under our old compound. She put the entire operation at risk with her actions."

"And was thoroughly chewed out over it," Faith put in.

"What are you suggesting?" Charity asked, focusing her attention on Honor.

"I'm not suggesting, I'm telling you that if we can't get with the program Roy and his team are part of, we should stay here."

"What? And miss all the fun?" Hope grunted dismissively. "Not on your life, sister. We were born to fight. Just because the Nameless Ones kept us on a short leash is no reason to hobble ourselves."

"Do you know what humans do to operatives who march to their own drummer?" Honor asked. "If you got really lucky, they'd just boot you out of this nice, cushy position in the CIA. Worst case, you'd end up with your ass in a cell."

"She's right." Hope spoke slowly. "Although the level of punishment would be determined by whether what we did actually harmed anyone on our side."

"Clap trap," Charity announced and poked Hope in the ribs. "Whose side are you on?"

"My own." Hope spoke with a simple dignity. "I know you don't trust Roy or Milton, but I think you overreacted when you dug into Milton's past. Not that it was right for you to do that in the first place."

"Fine." Charity bolted to her feet. "What a bunch of stars-in-your-eyes pussies you all are. See you at the meeting." She made a grab for her jacket and fled out the door.

Honor winced as it slammed, crashing against its stops.

"What the hell got into her?" Faith asked.

"I don't know," Hope replied thoughtfully. "She's progressively more paranoid the longer we're here. I've almost wondered if she's not having some kind of physical reaction to different food or a different environment."

"Is that even possible?" Honor asked.

Faith nodded gravely. "I worked with the geneticists. Charity might have been created with one of the less stable versions of V3 genes."

"Crap! Really?" At Faith's nod, Honor went on. "Is there any way to find out?" She got to her feet and began gathering the remains of their meal to take to the trash can.

"Sure," Faith said. "It'd be in that huge data dump Glory lifted."

"Do we have time to figure it out before whatever happens in…" Honor glanced at the microwave's clock, "twenty minutes at nineteen hundred?"

"Probably not," Faith said. "Let's figure out where Glory is and see if she can stop by here before the meeting."

Because Faith didn't bother to waste energy cloaking her telepathic sending, Honor heard her yell for Glory to, *Show up right now, goddammit.*

Honor rolled her eyes as she rinsed her hands at the kitchen sink. "That ought to get her attention."

Glory must've been close because a brisk knock rattled the door in less than five minutes. Faith let her in. "What the hell?" Glory looked from one woman to the other. Her face was flushed from hurrying to get there—or maybe she and Roy had taken advantage of their dinner break to do something other than eat.

"Shut the door," Honor said and built the best soundproofing she could around the room with mind power.

"What are you doing?" Glory asked. "Did you find other Nameless Ones close by?"

"Worse," Faith said.

"Okay." Glory perched on the edge of a couch. "Where's Charity? If it's that serious, shouldn't we all be here?"

"I'm switching to telepathic speech, and you should too," Hope announced. *"This is about Charity. She doesn't trust the men and wants us to plan our own offensive if we end up going to that West Virginia compound."*

Glory opened her mouth, but Honor waved her to silence. *"Hear us out. We don't have much time. And there's not much more to tell. Faith is worried Charity might be one of the unstable versions of the V3 configuration. You've got all those records in your head. Let us look. Or you can."*

"Sure. Help yourself. I'd look, but genetics aren't exactly my forte."

Faith moved next to Glory and took her hands. Physical contact made mind melds much easier. "Are you sure?" she mouthed. At Glory's nod, Faith closed her eyes.

Honor kept an eye on the clock as one minute passed, and then two. Before the third elapsed, Faith's eyes snapped open, and she let go of Glory. Her lips trembled, and she looked on the verge of tears.

"What?" All three of them practically screamed telepathically, the energy so violent, light flared around Faith.

"I didn't dig too deep..." Faith raked a hand through her black hair, *"because we don't have much time, but Charity came from the earliest V3 batch. Even worse, the egg and sperm combo that created her spent months in a deepfreeze before someone decided to reanimate it."*

"So she's at risk from two fronts?" Hope asked. *"Unstable chromosomes compounded by time in a freezer."*

Faith nodded slowly. "What are we going to do?" she asked out loud and looked from woman to woman.

"How bad is it likely to get? Can we salvage her?" Honor was shocked by the desperation in her mental voice and understood she didn't want to have to sacrifice any of them. Sudden pain flared behind her breastbone. They were sisters. A team. Surely there'd be some way to intervene.

"I'm thinking the same thing," Glory said quietly. *"Sorry for eavesdropping on your thoughts, Honor. My first choice is to try to handle this among us. If we tell the men, I'm afraid they'll stuff her in a cell."*

"And she'll just get angrier and angrier, and any chance we might have to turn this thing around will evaporate," Faith said. *"This could get very serious if we're not careful, and I don't want to lose her."*

"Define serious," Honor pressed.

"She could totally lose it. Become unpredictable. I saw it happen a time or two in the compound. You might not have because the geneticists locked them away." Faith winced and pained lines dug into the corners of her eyes.

Glory got to her feet. "We need to go, or we'll be late. If we're deployed to that compound near Keyser, we'll have to arrange things so two of us are always with her."

Honor joined her and moved slowly toward the door. Faith and Hope brought up the rear. None of them said anything, but a funereal pall hung over the group. If they couldn't redirect whatever was going on with Charity, they'd have to imprison her. Once that happened, she might retreat into madness and truly move beyond the possibility of salvage.

As if we didn't have enough problems.

Honor straightened her shoulders. No matter what, she'd do her best—even if it tore her heart out and left little chunks of her soul for carrion to feed on.

CHAPTER 4

Milton added a few lines to the strategic plan he'd drawn with the computer's simulation software and glanced at the men and women assembled in one of the smaller meeting rooms. "We'll strike fast and hard. Here." He moved the cursor to one spot in his schematic, which was projected onto a wall display. "And here." He tapped another. "Roy's team will provide a diversion while the women see if they can convince anyone to leave. Male or female. We're not discriminating this time. Frankly, I want to know if any of those amnesty broadcasts made it through to the masses."

"Do we have a Plan B in case it's a trap?" Charlie asked.

Milton cracked a grim smile. "We sure do. Two jet fighters will fly a pattern over the compound. If things turn to shit, you're to head for this concrete bunker." He tapped a few computer keys and brought up a satellite image of the compound. "I'm certain the freaks built it for the same reason: to have somewhere safe to retreat to."

"Don't you suppose it'll be locked?" David, another of Roy's team, asked. Like the others, his shaggy hair was coal black. Shrewd hazel eyes sparred with Milton.

"You're not thinking." Charity's voice dripped scorn. "Use those augmented brain cells to break in."

Color rose from the open neckline of David's black T-shirt, and he looked at the table. "Thanks," he mumbled. "You were born with that stuff. It's still pretty new for us."

"Be perceptive—or be dead," she countered.

Milton bit back a sharp retort and cast a sidelong glance at the woman. Her attitude had been downright snarky for the last week or so, and he didn't like the way she looked at him—as if he were yesterday's garbage. If he let his intuition rule, he'd order her back to her apartment and sort this out after tomorrow night's mission, but that might demoralize the other women...

Milton cleared his throat. "That'll be enough from you."

"Got it. Sir." Charity glowered at him from under lowered brows.

"Look sharp, everyone." Milton went on as if she hadn't said anything. "We'll leave before dawn, get into position during the afternoon, and strike at ten tomorrow night."

"Boss?" Roy's voice dragged Milton's gaze his way.

"Hold that thought, Kincaid." Milton trained his attention on Charity. "If you have doubts about this mission, let's get them out on the table now."

When she didn't respond, Hope poked her and hissed, "He's talking to you."

"Me?" Charity looked around. "What'd I do?"

The sunny smile she cast his way held such a false edge it unnerved him. For the barest moment, she looked more automaton than human.

"I said..." Milton cleared his throat, "if you have concerns about this mission, let's hear about them. Now."

"No. No concerns." She went back to studying her hands.

Milton looked at Roy. "What'd you want to say earlier?"

"Wasn't important." Roy caught and held Milton's gaze. Worry reflected from his eyes, but he obviously wasn't ready to voice his concerns.

"Okay," Milton growled, feeling anything but okay, "if we're clear about our roles, I have nothing further for you tonight. Get a decent night's sleep. Meet in the chopper bays at zero six hundred. Full combat gear."

Everyone stood and shuffled out of the room. An idea came to him. Before he could dissect his motives, Milton called, "Honor."

She turned. "Sir?"

"Stay put. I want to talk with you."

An uncomfortable look washed over her face, and he could've sworn she squared her shoulders. Charity waltzed past her and hissed something Milton couldn't hear into her ear. The discomfort on Honor's face shifted to something akin to disgust, and Milton's muscles tightened into rocks.

What the hell was going on?

Honor turned slowly and walked toward him, keeping her gaze downcast. She stopped two feet away and clasped her hands behind her, waiting. It wasn't like her to be meek. What was she hiding?

"You can't possibly be afraid of me. What's going on?" Milton drew back, shocked he'd asked such a personal question, and at why the answer mattered so much. Before she could say anything, he snapped, "Never mind. Follow me back to my office."

She did just that: followed him. She was light on her feet, catlike. If he didn't have some of her augmentation, which allowed him to sense energy fields, he wouldn't have been certain she was still there.

He placed his palm on the scanner mounted on the wall outside his door. His superiors had been after him to replace it with a retinal reader, but this seemed just as bulletproof to him. Once the door was open, he stood aside and motioned her in.

She stopped just inside the door. Quiet. Waiting. He intuited she'd done this before. Made herself as close to invisible as possible.

Still running on motives he wasn't willing to examine too

closely, Milton made his way to a cabinet at the rear of his office and pulled a bottle of Irish whiskey from it along with two glasses. He poured a healthy jot into both, set one on his desk, and walked the second one back to her.

She took the drink from him and continued to stand stock still. Edgy and silent.

"Have a drink," he suggested. "You look like you've had a rough day."

Honor raised her gaze, and he caught a glimpse of inexplicable sadness in the depths of her green eyes. "Thank you, sir." She took a cautious sip, gasping when the liquor hit first her tongue and then her throat.

"Didn't anyone drink in your compound?" He placed a hand under her elbow and pushed gently until she walked to a chair. "Go ahead," he urged. "Sit."

Honor dropped into the chair and took another swallow of whiskey, grimacing at the taste.

He hooked his foot around a second chair and positioned it so it faced hers. "Gets better with practice." He sat and reached for his own glass. Once he had it in hand, he took a long drink, sighing with pleasure as the fragrant liquid burned a path to his belly.

"I'm sure it does, sir. And no, women never had spirits in the compounds. The men did, but they never offered to share."

"Probably with good reason. If any of them had gotten shitfaced, you women might've ferreted out their secrets."

That brought a small smile to her generous mouth, and Milton understood how much he wanted to make her smile, wanted her to be relaxed in his presence, not this skittish bundle of nerves.

"Shitfaced means drunk, huh?" she asked.

He nodded. "Idioms passed you by too, huh?"

"Not all of them, but a lot. We watched movies, but the Nameless Ones decided which ones were acceptable. Ditto for our Internet time."

"Sometime, if things ever slow down, I'd like to hear more about how you lived before you came here."

She nodded. "Sure. It's not very interesting, but I'd be glad to tell you whatever you want to know."

It was an impossible lead-in to ignore. He set his glass on the edge of his desk and leaned toward her. "What I want to know right now is if you think we should include Charity in tomorrow's operation."

Because Milton never took his eyes from Honor's face, he saw the play of naked emotion before she smoothed her features to neutrality. Fear battled determination for ascendency in her expressive eyes.

She did look at him then, and he felt her weighing her words.

"The other women and I are worried about her too. We think she just needs more time to settle in."

"Why would she?" Milton asked. Even though it was far from second nature, he tried using his newly augmented senses to determine whether Honor was telling the truth.

"Well." Honor set her drink down. With her hands free, she steepled her fingers beneath her chin. "You're not all the same. Why would we be? There were differences, even among the genetic variations that formed us, so not all the V2s or V3s were alike. Along the same line of thought..." She plowed ahead, talking faster now. "We're concerned about this new V4 iteration. The infiltrator who almost nabbed Glory said he was V4. None of us had ever heard of such a thing before that."

If it was a ploy to divert him, it was smooth.

Honor looked at him from guileless eyes and asked, "Did you ever find out more about how they're different from us?"

"From a genome mapping perspective, yes." Milton drained more of his whiskey. "That was simple enough, since we had the dead guy to take tissue samples from and the rest of you to compare it with."

"What'd you find?" Honor took another cautious sip of her drink.

"It's not so much what we found, as being able to interpret what it means."

"Faith worked with the geneticists at the compound. Why not use her?" Honor drank more.

Thank Christ she seemed to be relaxing. Milton continued to watch Honor closely. "Because I had no idea what Faith did until right now. What about the rest of you?"

"Glory had special training to go on surveillance missions. Also, she's faster than most at linking to computer systems and draining them. Hope could double as a doctor. She's that good. Charity worked in the gardens and the kitchen. She's also a decent sleuth—good problem solving skills."

"What about you?" Milton leaned forward again. He wanted to untangle the enigma who sat across from him.

Honor laughed uncomfortably. "Oh, I was pretty much nobody. I couldn't keep my mouth shut, so I spent tons of time in an iso cell."

"But when you weren't there," he persisted.

"I designed mental weaponry."

"Define exactly what that means." He scooted his chair closer. Honor's alluring scent drew him, warm, piquant, and fresh. Her face was flushed from the alcohol, and strands of long black hair escaped her braids, curling around her face.

"I helped some of us determine how to use mind power to kill. We can also link our mental abilities."

"Like a Vulcan mind meld?" Incredulity raced through him as he wondered if the men who'd had the injections could do the same thing.

"Probably, with training." She answered his unspoken question.

Milton snapped to attention. It wasn't what he'd asked. "Probably with training, what?" he asked carefully.

"Aw, crap." The color deepened across her high cheek bones. "Busted. I'm sorry. I didn't mean to help myself to your thoughts, but when you're this close to me, it's almost impossible not to hear them."

Heat traveled from his stomach upward. How many more of his thoughts had she intercepted?

"Practically all of them." She gazed askance at him, but the corners of her mouth twitched into a half-smile.

It was rare for him to feel uncomfortable, but losing the privacy of his mind was a huge nut to accept. "Back to Charity," he said, his voice gruff with awkwardness.

"How about this?" Honor finished her drink and twirled the glass between her hands. "The other women and I are on top of things. We'll make sure nothing…unexpected happens."

"What if I pull rank and order her to stay here?" he demanded, not liking her answer.

Honor shook her head. "That'd be a bad idea." After a pause, she added hastily, "Sir. With all due respect."

Milton chortled. "You're learning. Why is it a bad idea?"

Honor closed her teeth over her lower lip. "Like all of us, she's finding her way. Figuring out where she fits in here. Even though we lived in the western United States, we may as well have been in Bangladesh for all the differences between living here and where we were after the rebellion."

"You still haven't told me why it's a bad idea."

"She needs to trust you. If you ride herd on her, treat her like the Nameless Ones treated us, she never will, and this…problem of hers will just get worse."

Desperation flared, a glowing nimbus she nipped quickly, but he'd been paying close attention, plus he'd been inside her mind. Milton pushed forward with a combination of intuition and his augmented ability. "You're worried it will get worse anyway."

Her gaze skittered away. "Yes. No. Possibly. These things are hard to predict. Please." She leaned forward this time and placed a hand over his where it lay atop his leg. "Let us handle it our way. I give you my word we'll ask for help before it gets out of control."

Her touch was warm, electric. Before he could stop himself, he set his other hand over hers, and turned the bottom hand upward, capturing her flesh between his. His mouth was suddenly dry, and his groin tightened with a rush of sexual energy so intense it stole his breath.

Words became a struggle, but he forced them out anyway. "Doesn't sound very smart to me. Is there any chance she'll switch allegiance?"

Honor's eyes widened. "Oh hell, no. You mean fight for the Nameless Ones?" When Milton nodded, she was even more emphatic. "No. That'd never happen. She hates them just as much as we do."

It was the main thing that had worried him: that he'd been playing host to a double agent—again. Some of the tension drained out of him, and he rubbed his fingers over Honor's where they lay clasped between his.

"I really should go, sir." She tried to pull her hand back, but he didn't let go.

"Do you always do what you should?"

Honor looked away. "Not a fair question, sir."

"Stop calling me that!"

"But you are my commanding officer." Honor kept her voice soft, but the meaning in her words slapped Milton squarely across his forehead.

He released her hand. "Sorry." He spoke stiffly. "I forgot myself. You're free to go."

The sadness he'd sensed earlier was back in spades. It flowed from her in slow, tired waves. He pushed, surprised when she let him inside her mind. Not far, but enough for him to view the loneliness she'd lived with all her life. Her only safety zone had been the dozen women in her dorm at the compound, and seven of them were dead. No wonder she needed to do everything possible to protect Charity.

Milton got to his feet and offered her a hand. She took it and stood too. "Thanks for helping me understand you a little," he said.

"You're welcome. Sometimes that way is easier than talking. Thank you for not insisting Charity stay here."

"She's important to you," he said. "I didn't fully appreciate how much you depend on each other until you allowed me into your thoughts."

Milton didn't know if he moved toward her, she toward him, or both of them simultaneously, but Honor ended up in his arms. He tightened his hold, enjoying the feel of her sleekly muscled body against his. She matched his six-foot height and fit perfectly in his arms. His cock hardened against her belly, and her eyes widened in surprise.

"Of course you'd be a virgin," he murmured, stroking his hands down her back.

"We were off-limits to the Nameless Ones, but we talked about sex among ourselves."

Arousal flashed deep inside him. Even though he knew he shouldn't, he asked, "What did you talk about?" He cupped his hands around her high, firm buttocks and snugged her against his erection.

Desire apparently trumped discomfort, and she pushed against him. "Men. We talked about how penises get hard, and how one might feel inside us." She licked her lips, and heat flickered in her eyes. "Sometimes we'd touch ourselves and mind link, so we could feel each other come."

He'd never considered that possible use for his enhanced senses. The feedback loop from feeling what his partner felt right along with his own arousal intrigued him and made him hotter than hell. Honor pressed closer against him and kneaded his back.

Milton traced her full lower lip with his thumb. "Has anyone told you what a devilishly attractive woman you are?"

She shook her head.

He couldn't resist the siren call of those lips. Milton angled his head and closed his mouth over hers. He kept the kiss tentative in case he wasn't reading her signals right, but she ran her tongue over his mouth, tasting him. He licked, nibbled, sucked, and she kissed him back with growing fervor as her body radiated need. Her nipples hardened where they pressed into his chest, and she rubbed against his ridiculously erect cock.

About the time she pushed her tongue into his mouth, and he sparred with it, loving the taste of her, common sense intruded. He pulled back, his breath coming unevenly. He wanted to strip her clothes off, unwrap her, worship the amazing body he'd scuffled with in the gym, but tonight wasn't the time. Not before a major offensive, and not with her in a direct line of command, with him functioning as her team leader. The women ended up his responsibility to remove Glory from reporting to Roy, but here was the same problem all over again.

Reluctantly, he placed his hands on either side of her head. "Honor, we can't do this."

"I know it's wrong, but I've never been kissed before, and I…" She looked away. "…didn't want it to end. I'm sorry, sir. I'll do a better job of—"

"Goddammit, Honor. You're not listening." Frustration vied with desire and feeling like a shit for letting the situation get out of hand in the first place.

"Yes I am. You said what we did was wrong."

"No, I didn't, but the timing's bad." He paused a beat. "And you work for me, which means—"

"I know exactly what it means. I may have been sequestered in that compound, but I'm far from stupid." She wrenched away from him and stumbled toward the door.

"Honor, please."

She spun to face him. "This was a mistake." Hurt carved furrows around her eyes. "I'm used to being by myself. Taking care of myself. Don't worry. I won't be a burden on you."

"That's not what I—"

She turned and fled out the door. Milton considered going after her, but recognized it was a bad idea. The attraction between them was so strong, there'd be no way to have a rational conversation.

Until they'd shared an orgasm or two.

He reached down and rearranged his straining cock to a better position. It leaped into his hand, and he considered jacking off. He was so aroused, it wouldn't take more than a few strokes. He strode to the door to make certain it was well and truly shut before he went around to the large chair behind his desk.

Sinking into it, he freed himself from the confines of his trousers and shut his eyes. His hand moved on his shaft with practiced ease, and he imagined thrusting into Honor, taking her, making her his. Sperm boiled hot at the base of his balls, and he barely grabbed a handful of tissues in time to catch the flood that spurted from him.

onor raced out the door of Milton's office and ignored the elevator, choosing the stairwell instead. Her body was on fire from his touch. Leaving him was one of the hardest things she'd ever done.

But I didn't leave him. He pulled away from me. Maybe he doesn't want me as much as I want him.

The more she thought about it, the truer it felt. He'd had women —probably lots of them in addition to his three wives. He was experienced, and whatever sparked between them hadn't been enough to knock him off his feet. He'd been aroused. She'd sensed it, smelled it, and felt the obvious when it prodded her, but it wasn't enough to make him throw caution to the winds.

She let herself out the building door, and icy air hit her overheated face. Unfortunately, it didn't change the welter of doubts pummeling her.

Her clit throbbed painfully, rubbing against her wet panties.

"Where are you? What'd you tell him?" Blasted into her head.

Charity.

"I'm outside, and I didn't tell him a thing. What the hell were you

thinking I'd tell him, anyway?" Thwarted arousal made her surly. Rather than head for her apartment, where Charity was likely to bang on the door until she opened it, Honor broke into a run. She dialed in her night vision and jumped obstacles as they reared in front of her.

"You sound bitchy. What happened? Did lover boy turn you down?"

"Go fuck yourself, Charity. Leave me alone." Honor slapped wards in place to impede further attempts to communicate. She ran harder, heading for the perimeter fence, determined to use physical activity to wipe Milton's beautiful dark eyes and starkly-boned face from her mind.

It didn't work.

Finally, she ducked behind thick shrubbery, stuffed a hand deep in her pants, and rubbed her swollen nub. There was nothing elegant about her movements. Need drove her, pure and simple. An orgasm followed seconds later, so intense it made her legs rubbery, but at least she could think again. With her breath rasping roughly, making clouds in the icy night air, she set herself to rights and wended her way back to her apartment.

If luck was with her, she wouldn't see any of the other women until tomorrow morning. She needed alone time to set some defenses. Milton would be coming with them on tomorrow's operation. She'd have to keep her guard up, pretend nothing happened between them. The men couldn't know. Neither could the women. It wasn't anything like Glory and Roy. He'd rescued her from sure death at the hands of the Nameless Ones in a killer snowstorm.

She didn't need anything even close to that dramatic from Milton.

Do I only want his body?

She turned the question over as she walked and didn't care much for her answer. It would be ever so much easier if her attraction to Milton was purely physical, but she admired his mind, enjoyed listening to him, talking with him.

Not good, Honor, she lectured herself. *Never show weakness. Needing anyone is weakness. Someone could discover that vulnerability and exploit it to control me.*

Strong words. Easy to say, harder to stick with. She let herself into her building. The guard nodded her way. She inclined her head and forced a smile before making her way to her apartment. Mercifully, no one was waiting inside to intercept her. She undressed mechanically, hanging things as she went. After a quick, very hot shower, she crawled under the quilt on her bed. Having the thick quilt and several pillows still felt like an incredible luxury. At the compound, she'd been limited to one thin blanket and a single lumpy pillow.

She turned onto her side and shut her eyes. Milton flared behind her closed lids with his upper lip curved in his trademark sardonic grin, and her heart clenched. He was such a beautiful man, more perfect than anyone had a right to be.

"I have to stop thinking like that," she muttered and picked through the circuitry that fired her brain, rearranging as she went. She pushed some things to the fore, and buried her feelings for Milton as deep as she could. It was the only way to scrub him from her mind. She'd wanted him before tonight, but what had leaped to life between them would undermine her control if she couldn't get a firm handle on it.

At length, once she'd done everything she could think of, she turned her mind to sleep mode, gratified when darkness descended. She'd been afraid her brain, which was becoming more human as she spent time around them, would defy her command.

Honor woke at the time she'd programmed and got ready on autopilot. If she kept herself focused on their mission, and her link to the other women, she might be able to get through the next two days without sinking into a funk over Milton's rejection. She walked through her equipment list, double checking she had everything. Once she was as ready as she could be, she strode out the door. There was time for breakfast, but she didn't feel hungry.

A brisk run solidified her resolve, and she strolled into the launch area with a few minutes to spare. Milton greeted her with a warm smile that did funny things to her insides. She looked away and mumbled her good mornings, trying not to look at him and failing miserably.

"Did you sleep well?" He walked to her side and tried to establish eye contact.

"Yes, sir. Fine, sir. Thank you for asking. Sir."

When he stared at her, his expression shading from shock to disappointment to something she couldn't interpret, she asked, "Permission to get the remainder of my kit, sir?"

At his curt nod, she headed for the Kevlar vests and the firearms. She usually carried a 9 mm semiautomatic Sig Sauer sidearm, and an assault rifle. Those varied, but today the arms master, a man who looked to be in his mid-forties with sandy hair and sharp blue eyes, handed her an AK-47 Kalashnikov. She hefted it, testing its balance, and took ammo rounds and a body belt to hold them.

Roy and Glory came into the hangar arm in arm. Honor told herself to look away, but she didn't avert her gaze fast enough. The love clinging to them knifed her somewhere south of her heart. She wanted someone to look at her the way Roy looked at Glory, as if she were the most perfect, precious gift in the world.

"For Christ's fucking sake," she muttered. "I've got to stop feeling sorry for myself."

"What was that, agent?" The arms master quirked a brow and swept a speculative gaze up and down her body.

"Nothing important. Do I have everything?"

"Everything from my station," he concurred and shifted his attention to his stash of rifle scopes.

"Thanks." She walked to the open door at the far end of the hangar and eyed the large, black helicopter waiting for them. It was one of the double rotor models, and they swung slowly as the engines idled.

She felt Faith, Hope, and Charity when they entered the hangar, their energy distinct enough she didn't have to turn around. Roy's team followed hard on their heels. The women collected their field gear and flanked her.

"You got here early," Charity observed with a catty undertone beneath her bland words.

"Not very," Honor said and turned to look at the other woman. She hated not trusting her. It went against the grain. She'd left a world where the women in her dorm were the only ones she could trust. Having that change felt wrong—on many levels.

"Still a wee bit out of sorts, I see." Charity grinned at her. "You should borrow a page from me."

"How's that?"

When Charity didn't answer, Hope leaned close. "We think she found someone to screw last night, but she's not telling us much."

Honor clamped her jaw into a tight line. "Not the time or place for that discussion. We need to focus, or we'll end up dead." She slung her rifle over a shoulder.

"You asked." Hope shot a hurt look her way.

Honor wrapped an arm around Hope and gave her a quick, hard hug. "So I did. Sorry."

Milton strode to them. "Let's get cracking." He clapped his hands together once. "Go. Last five seats in the bird are yours."

"Where will you be?" Charity asked, and the inflection in her voice struck a sexualized note that curdled Honor's stomach. Had Charity sought out Milton last night? Worse, had he found her more irresistible than he'd found Honor?

"Flying the bird," he said curtly and jogged past them, taking the steps into the chopper two at a time.

Because she was desperate to know if anything had happened between them, even something Milton might be kicking himself for now, Honor pushed toward Charity's mind and then his. Both were closed—at least to her, which catapulted her suspicions into high gear.

Feeling glum, angry, and like Milton had played her for a sucker —never mind her role in this fucked up mess—she stalked toward the chopper, more determined than ever to bury her emotions six feet under. Having her human side plucked raw sucked, and she reached for emotional neutrality. Usually it was easy to latch onto, but not today.

"Something wrong, hon?" Glory took the seat next to hers and buckled in.

"Why would you ask?" Honor strapped in as well.

Glory twisted to look her right in the eyes. "Because tension is streaming off you in buckets."

"Maybe I'm nervous about what we're doing."

"Let's try that one again." Glory shifted to telepathic speech, and Honor felt the shielding the other woman built around it.

"Let's not."

"If you're worried about Charity—"

Honor took a deep breath, blew it out, and followed it with another one. *"Speaking of which, do we have a plan to keep an eye on her?"*

Glory nodded. *"We do. We talked about it some more last night."*

"Without me?" Honor felt thunderstruck. How could they have left her out of something that important?

"You weren't there." Glory answered her unspoken thoughts, and Honor did a more thorough job shielding her mind.

"Did you even try to find me?" Honor swallowed a hefty dose of outrage. Not only was she not attractive enough to tempt Milton... Even the women found her so unimportant, they'd moved forward without consulting her.

Half a smile curved Glory's mouth, and she shook her head. *"I told them to leave you be. I guess I was hoping..."* She let her words trail off.

"Well, don't bother." Honor spoke aloud—trying to modulate the sour inflection in her tone and failing—before she switched back to telepathy. *"What'd you come up with for Charity?"*

"Not much more than our earlier discussion. Two of us with her at all times—no matter what."

"Do you think you should let Milton know that?" Honor asked. *"In case he has some kind of battle plan that would deploy us differently."*

"Why can't you let him know?"

Honor shook her head. Glory's discerning gaze bit deep, but she didn't say anything further. Maybe if Honor didn't weaken and talk about her ragged emotional state, it would go away—or at least fade into enough of a background role to leave her in peace.

"Sorry, hon." Glory patted her hand.

Honor jerked away. "Don't do that," she hissed. "We're machines, remember? We don't do things like sorry."

Compassion filled Glory's green eyes, the emotion so bittersweet it felt alive, skittering across the few inches between them. Looking at her friend almost undid her, and Honor turned her gaze forward. She recited mathematical computations under her breath to scrub anything nonessential from her mental processes.

MILTON SETTLED HEAVILY onto the left seat of the helicopter's controls. When Roy let himself into the cockpit and took up the right seat, Milton grunted to acknowledge his presence.

"Anything wrong?" Roy's tone held a studied nonchalance.

"Not a thing. Why?"

"It seems like you might've changed your mind—or something," Roy said. "Except I guess that's not it, since you just cleared us for takeoff."

"I don't pay you to have opinions," Milton growled.

"You don't pay me to be your friend either, but I am. What the fuck happened between last night and right now?"

"Why do you think anything happened?" Milton countered, not wanting zip shit to do with this conversation, but unwilling to totally pull rank and tell Kincaid to mind his own business. He engaged the throttle and kept his eye on the gauges. The next volley of words between them was pilot and copilot going through standard takeoff protocol prior to leaving the ground.

Roy remained silent for a while after that. Long enough Milton began to hope he'd given up on his earlier line of questioning.

After they passed through ten thousand feet, Roy said, "I think something happened because you're as out of sorts as a hooker in a gold rush town after the miners moved on for greener pastures."

"That's a hell of an analogy, Kincaid." Milton snorted in spite of himself.

"Does that mean you're going to tell me what happened?"

"Christ! You're worse than a temperamental game show host with a question deficit."

Roy laughed. "Nope, just an attorney. We go to law school because we love asking questions. By the way, your analogy was almost as good as mine."

"The CIA should take better advantage of your law degree."

"You're hedging." Roy exhaled noisily. "What I think happened..." He made a course correction, feeding new data into the three-axis autopilot. "...is you had some sort of skirmish with Honor—"

"Hold up right there." Milton let go of the cyclic and turned in his seat to look at Roy. "My personal life is none of your business."

"Don't see why not," Roy retorted. "You've done a fair job burying yourself in mine."

Touché.

Milton thought about it. On one level, it'd be a relief to at least hear what Roy thought. After all, he'd hooked up with a woman like Honor. Furthermore, Roy and Glory's relationship appeared to be working. Maybe he'd be able to shed some light on Milton's dilemma.

He rested his hand on the controls again and cleared his throat. "You're correct. About Honor."

"What about Honor?" Roy prodded. "That tells me less than nothing, other than that my intuition was spot on."

"For fuck's sake, stop being a lawyer. I'm not some rube for you to grill on the stand."

Roy rolled his eyes. "Let's cut to the chase. Did you sleep with her?"

"Of course not. She works for me."

"Hey!" Roy jabbed him in the ribs. "Spare me. I remember that bimbo who worked for you in Kabul."

"That was different," Milton sputtered. "She wasn't a field agent."

"You're splitting hairs." Roy cast a knowing grin Milton's way. "The genetically altered women can be incredible in bed."

"I wouldn't know."

"Oh ho! So that's the problem. Did she shoot you down?"

"If you'd shut up for long enough, I'll tell you." Milton unclenched his fist from around the cyclic. The helicopter stopped jittering in the air, probably because he'd removed his heavy hand from her controls.

Roy folded his hands over the cyclic on his side and said, "My bird. You talk."

"...and so, once I halfway came to my senses, I told her we couldn't keep going, at least not last night in my office. She took it wrong..." Breath steamed from between his clenched teeth. "...and stormed out of my office. I know I hurt her feelings. Christ, she all but offered herself to me."

"I'm sure you can patch things up," Roy said.

"You haven't heard everything." Milton forced the next words out. "I was on my way out the door, heading for my base quarters for the night, when Charity busted onto the scene. Damn if she didn't throw herself into my arms and plaster her mouth all over mine."

"What'd you do?"

"Pulled her off and told her to leave immediately, but all she did was give me that arch, little, shit-eating grin of hers and say that she knew things hadn't gone well between me and Honor, and she was the consolation prize." Milton shook his head. "What the fuck? Did Honor run out of my office and blab to her buddies about me?"

Roy made another course correction. When he spoke, his tone was thoughtful. "She doesn't seem like the gossipy type. Charity could've plucked some things from her mind, unless Honor had her mental shields up."

"Mmph. Hadn't thought of that."

"Did Charity leave when you told her to?"

"Not right away, but after I repeated myself twice, she stopped unbuttoning her shirt and stormed away—kind of a repeat of what Honor did, minus the shirt."

"Glory told me some of the women's concerns about Charity. No detail, only that they had a plan to make sure she can't do any damage. When I asked for specifics, she shook her head." Roy paused a beat. "When she does that, I've learned there's no point in pressing for more."

Milton stared out the windscreen and shook his head. "I should've made Charity remain at Langley. Every instinct I have said it was the right thing to do."

"Why didn't you?"

"Because Honor begged me. She's worried about Charity too and inferred I'd push her over some sort of one-way cliff into a place she wouldn't be salvageable."

"Compassion isn't a curse, but Charity's not sounding very stable."

Milton observed his old friend with a gimlet eye. "You'd better hope I live long enough to not regret my decision. Now let's firm up our ground strategy."

"I still think it'd be easy enough to make things up with Honor—" Roy began.

"Later, Kincaid. We should be in position by eighteen hundred. I want fifteen minute plans from that point."

"You got it, boss." Roy jimmied a tablet from his flight suit and made notations on its slick surface.

CHAPTER 6

*H*onor crouched in a thick stand of eucalyptus trees a few miles north of Keyser, West Virginia. By her calculations, their objective was five hundred yards to the southeast. The chopper dumped them hours before, and they'd spent the intervening time—once Roy and Milton parceled out who was doing what—jogging through muddy, overgrown terrain so inhospitable she'd ended up belly crawling more than once. The front of her camo pants and top were smeared with thick, slimy mud, and she'd used more of the stuff to black out her face. It had been dark for hours, and it was closing on twenty-two hundred—the time they were supposed to attack.

She understood why the bird hadn't delivered them closer to their target—safer for everyone that way—and the exertion had done more than anything else she might've ginned up to clear her mind of everything but the task ahead. She thought about others in the compound and hoped at least a few would chose to switch allegiance. It should be a no-brainer for the women—except it hadn't worked at her home compound in the Pacific Northwest, so it might not work that way here, either.

The chittering howl of a pack of coyotes rose unnervingly close, before the eerie sound was taken up by another bunch farther away.

"It'll be good to get moving." Glory drew even with her and hunkered on her haunches.

"No shit."

"Did the Nameless Ones ever send you on any missions?" Curiosity underscored Glory's question.

"No. Remember, I worked behind the scenes sharpening our mental weaponry." Honor hesitated. "It was a one-on-one thing, interplay between the computer part of our minds and our more human abilities."

Glory teetered before catching herself with a hand and repositioned her feet. "So you figured out how to make us more effective?"

Honor nodded. "Even though the Nameless Ones never actually sent me into the thick of things, I got to hear how my strategies and ideas worked whenever someone came back. Sometimes I'd mind link to them while they were in the field—if they were close enough." She paused a beat. This was one more thing she'd never been able to discuss openly before, and it still didn't feel quite right.

Faith, Hope, and Charity joined them.

"Whew!" Faith rolled her eyes. "Caught my ankle in a submerged mass of branches."

"Are you all right?" Glory glanced at her.

"Yeah. Charity calmed me down." Faith grimaced. "Actually she bitch slapped me, but it did the trick. I quit panicking and started thinking."

"You never did thank me," Charity muttered, but Faith shot her a look and rubbed her jaw, presumably where the other woman hit her.

"Where's Roy's team?" Hope asked.

"Right behind you." David spoke low as he slipped into view.

"You weren't always," Hope countered.

"Boss assigned us a different route." Charlie slid from the shadows, joining them. "Makes sense—in case one group was apprehended, it wouldn't blow the whole operation right out of the gate."

Much as the women looked alike, the men did too, but they cheated with black hair dye since they didn't have genetic manipulation on their side. All of them were tall and muscular, damn near identical in their field duds.

Honor glanced about, wondering where Milton and Roy were. Almost as if they were tuned in to her thoughts, they came into view, moving low to the ground, followed by the other four men on Roy's team.

Milton moved from one woman to the next, touching shoulders, and murmuring quiet encouragement. When he got to Honor, he said, "No mercy. If you hesitate, they'll kill you."

He positioned himself so he faced all of them and added, "It doesn't feel right not going in with you, but I don't want to jeopardize your chances for success."

Honor nodded. They'd hashed this one out. More than once. His human energy field would stick out like a lion in a sheep pen and could easily compromise what they were trying to accomplish.

"We'll be fine," she mumbled and worked to project a certainty she didn't quite feel.

Milton gave her a curt thumbs up and motioned Roy's men close. *"Everyone clear what their job is?"* His telepathic speech was mildly distorted, probably because he wasn't used to communicating that way. *"Last chance to ask questions."*

When no one said anything, he pointed to his wrist computer. *"We'll set up the diversion. It'll blow twenty minutes past the top of the hour. You women have to be clear by then, along with anyone willing to come with you. Got it?"*

Honor nodded and traded glances with the four women. They'd split into two teams. She, Glory, and Charity in one, and Faith and Hope in the other. According to intel Roy gleaned from the last compound, women were housed in four pods. Her group would hit two, giving each five minutes to exit the building. If they met any Nameless Ones along the way, they'd be offered a quick choice.

Join us or die.

Her mouth was dry, and bile burned the back of her throat when her stomach contracted. Honor tried to subdue the physical symptoms of nervousness with reason, but it didn't work very well. She still felt like crap.

"Same thing happened to me," Glory hissed in her ear. "That one mission the Nameless Ones sent me on, I was nervous as a feral cat."

"What about the night you freed us?" Honor whispered back.

Glory twisted her mouth into a wry grin. "That was easier."

"Why?"

"Because you were my friends, and I hoped I could save all of you."

"Maintain silence." Milton sent a disapproving glance their way. "Telepathic speech only once you leave this clearing. Use your communicators as a last resort."

"Meet back here at twenty two forty," Roy reminded them. "Move out. Now."

The men faded deeper into the eucalyptus grove. It was time. No more excuses. They had a job to do. Glory jerked her chin in the direction the men had gone, and all five of them followed. Once they were closer, her team of three would veer right to access the southeast side of the compound. The other two women would circle round the back. Honor hoped this compound was laid out the same way as the one she'd lived in. It was supposed to be, but if it wasn't, it'd be a neat trick to be in and out as fast as they had to be.

The night was as close to black as night ever got. Thick cloud cover obscured both moon and stars. Honor's heart rattled against her ribs, and she worked to control her breathing. If she could slow it down, maybe her heart would stop banging about. No one said a word, but she sensed the other four women's energy like a banner against the Nameless Ones' oppression. For the barest moment, she allowed herself to feel hopeful.

Charity might be a wildcard, but she'd never jeopardize the mission.

Honor was as certain of that as she'd ever been of anything.

All too soon, the compound came into view. Faith and Hope raced toward the rear intent on finding a window they could jimmy and crawl through. Her team moved from one patch of shadows to the next, communicating with hand signals. The Nameless Ones might intercept telepathy.

Glory settled beneath a window and sent a jolt of energy to unlock it. The three of them crouched motionless, waiting to see if a silent alarm triggered a greeting party. Honor pushed outward with her hyper-tuned senses, feeling for danger, and dialed in her night vision.

Nothing concrete bounced back to her, but the fine hairs on the back of her neck prickled. She forced herself to hold her ground, while her imagination worked overtime. A minute dripped past, followed by half of another. When nothing happened, Glory motioned them forward.

Reaching upward, she grasped the edges of the windowsill and swung her body up and sideways until her foot caught the sill, and she disappeared from view. Honor followed her. The rifle over her shoulder made what should've been an easy gymnastic maneuver much harder than she expected, until she rearranged the rifle's stock so its weight didn't work against her. The drop on the other side was farther than she expected. She bent her knees to take up the shock of landing and crouched next to Glory in what looked like a storeroom.

So far so good.

They waited, but Charity didn't vault through the opening.

"Crap!" Glory mouthed the word and stood upright. She grasped the windowsill with her fingers and pulled her body to eye level with the high window before dropping next to where Honor waited. The next word she mouthed was, "Gone."

Fuck! How could she?

Worse, why was I so certain she'd never do anything to jeopardize us all?

Glory gestured toward the window. Honor glanced at her watch and shook her head. They had to move now if they were going to sweep the compound. Their only other choice was to go after Charity, and that was such a breach of protocol, Honor couldn't square it with herself. She made *let's go* motions with both hands and saw Glory's curt nod. The two of them cracked the door, peering out cautiously. It led to a very familiar looking corridor, twin to one in their home compound.

Perhaps because their brains were mechanized, the Nameless Ones had come up with a design for their compounds and simply repeated it over and over. It made sense. Once you learned one layout, it was good everywhere. Saved a lot of time and wasted energy.

Honor sent a short burst of power to turn the cameras that lined the halls upward. She followed Glory to the door of what should be one of the women's dorms. Unlike her home compound, her palm wouldn't open this door. By the time she got there, Glory had blown the locking mechanism with kinetics, and Honor followed her into the room, pushing the door shut behind her.

Blanket-covered lumps lined the beds. Glory started forward, but Honor grabbed her shoulder. Something wasn't right. At least one of the women—probably more than that—should've wakened when the door opened. They weren't programmed to sleep that deeply, and certainly not through unexpected noises. It was a risk because someone might intercept her energy, but she threw her augmented senses open enough to determine what had happened.

Shock registered, and before she could stop herself, she gasped. "Dead. They're all dead."

Glory's eyes widened. She covered the distance to the first bed in two quick strides and twitched the blanket aside. A single bullet hole between the woman's eyes stared back at them.

The reality of what the dead women meant nearly flattened

Honor. Protocol be damned, she risked mind speech. *"So they were expecting us. It's a trap."*

Glory stopped mid-step and spun to face Honor, as she deployed her own power. Honor saw it spiral outward, testing for any life beyond their own in the room. Her face scrunched with pain. *"Do you suppose there's any point in checking the other dorm?"*

Honor shook her head. The women in the room hadn't been dead long, not even an hour, since their bodies retained heat. *"The Nameless Ones figured out we were close and did this to prove a point. That they still run things."*

"We've got to get out of here." Glory started for the door and twisted the latch, but it didn't budge.

Honor raced to her side. The trap they'd suspected had snapped shut—with them inside its jaws. Together they focused their mental power on the lock, willing it to yield, but nothing happened. Her chest tight with dread, Honor reached for her pistol intent on decimating door and lock. Before she got the gun out of its holster, the door burst open, and half a dozen Nameless Ones surged into the room.

"Shit!" Glory backed up until she was shoulder to shoulder with Honor.

One particularly burly man stepped forward. "Nice of you to drop in, girls. As you can see, we're a bit shy of women just now."

"Bastards!" Glory's face twisted in horror and outrage. "Why'd you have to kill them? They never harmed you."

"Now how the hell would you have any way of knowing that?" another man snarled and switched his attention to the other men. "Let's get them into iso cells. Then we can go after the rest."

Honor pushed power as hard as she could, trying for maximum damage, but the men were so well shielded, her energy boomeranged back, zapping her. The leader brayed laughter. "Nice try, girlie. We mind-linked with the men in your home compound before they died. You've got a few sins to atone for."

"Not nearly as many as you do," Honor countered, filled with helpless fury.

Glory ducked halfway behind her. It seemed out of character for her to hide from anything, but the boom of her gun explained everything and nearly deafened Honor. One of the men went down in a fountain of crimson that spattered the walls and floor. Ashamed she'd forgotten about her own weapons, Honor shouldered the Kalashnikov and sprayed the remaining men, cutting them to ribbons of gristle and bone where they stood.

Apparently their orders had been to capture her and Glory alive because none of them made the slightest effort to defend themselves. Honor stared at the grisly scene and wiped blood out of her eyes, not quite believing what she'd done.

Glory tugged hard on Honor's arm. "Let's go! You're just standing there gawking."

Honor dragged herself away from the dead bodies sprawled at unnatural angles in pools of blood. Despite knowing how, she'd never actually killed before. Starting with her own kind was so harsh, she couldn't think about it. Never mind she hated the Nameless Ones. Still they were her kin. Far more like her than normal humans ever could be.

A quick glance up and down the hall showed nothing but empty space. Why wasn't the enforcer branch of the Nameless Ones pelting toward them *en masse*? They were all mind-linked. Surely they knew their companions lay dead on the floor of the women's dorm.

A muted blast sounded far away. Fear lent her speed, and she bolted after Glory back through the storeroom and out the window. Honor tried to tuck and roll, but she landed hard. Breath whooshed from her lungs, and the rifle dug painfully into her side. Five more blasts, louder this time, rocked the ground, and fire blazed skyward, lighting the night. An unsettling rumble crackled next to her ears. The building reverberated ominously. Cracks formed in the concrete.

"Get up!" Glory yanked on her arms. Honor lurched to her feet and broke into a shambling run, following the other woman into heavy timber fifty yards away. Behind them, the building crumpled in on itself. A gas main must've burst because flames shot a long way above them.

"Sorry," Honor said once they were behind a huge, spreading oak tree. "Thanks for dragging me out of there."

"Are you all right?" Glory grabbed her face and made Honor look at her.

"Physically. Let's not talk about the rest."

"Wasn't going to. Do you suppose Faith and Hope got out?" Glory shoved her semiautomatic handgun back in its shoulder holster. "And where the fuck did Charity run off to?"

Honor draped the rifle's harness back over her body. "Guess there was a reason for us to learn to shoot after all." She pushed back hysteria, forcing an icy calm. "Do you think it'd be okay for us to use telepathy to locate the others?"

"No. I have a feeling the Nameless Ones didn't all die in the explosion, and it would give them a direct bead on our location—if they're listening, and they pretty much have to be." She squinched her eyes in thought. "Twenty two forty was two minutes ago. I say we go to the rendezvous."

Because she didn't have a better plan, Honor fell into step next to Glory. Nothing had gone according to plan tonight.

Nothing.

Why am I so surprised? I know next to nothing about covert missions.

There'd been plenty of hard fighting during the rebellion seven years before, but she'd been too young to be a part of it, only fifteen when she'd been displaced from her breeding farm and moved to the Pacific Northwest compound where she'd spent the next seven years.

Maybe because her guard was down, an image of the dozen dead women in the dorm pummeled her. Honor cringed before pure, cold anger straightened her spine with determination. The women had been gunned down in cold blood for no reason other than to create an object lesson. The Nameless Ones could've tossed them in iso cells, or used straw dummies in the beds, or hidden in the beds themselves. Their use of violence was so casual, it turned her blood to a cascade of icicles.

No reason for me to feel bad about killing them.

None at all.

Their willingness to sacrifice their own rang such a coldblooded note, she wondered if she'd ever known the Nameless Ones at all—despite working side by side with them for years. If they were callous enough to do that, what hope could she and the other women—even aided by the CIA—possibly have?

We're doomed. They'll kill us all because they're willing to do the unspeakable.

Honor shook herself. She'd never had any hope. Not really. The small respite since Glory had rescued them was just a blip on the radar screen. She was a soldier. Cannon fodder. She'd fight until they killed her. Not worth sifting through how she felt about anything. She was a machine, goddammit. Feelings were for normal humans.

Questions rose in a corner of her mind about the others. What had happened to Roy and Milton? To Charlie and David and the rest of Roy's team?

It doesn't matter.

Her mind voice was so ruthless, she scarcely recognized it as belonging to herself. Once it had her full attention, it added. *We'll fight until there aren't any of us left. End of story.*

"That's odd." Glory's harsh whisper grated in Honor's ear, dragging her out of the bleak place her mind had become. "These are the right coordinates, but no one else is here."

CHAPTER 7

Once the last of the Semtex and C4 charges detonated, Milton caught Roy's eye and mimed pulling a respirator into place. Roy would understand it was a signal to move out and sweep the facility with the rest of his team. Milton headed in the opposite direction to check on the women. He'd wanted to go with them—they were his responsibility after all—but the logistics of masking his energy from the freaks had been too difficult. Not much point in him being there if he added to the risk of discovery by broadcasting his humanness. Plus Honor and Glory convinced him they'd be fine for the short time until they regrouped at the rendezvous point.

He was a few minutes late because one of the charges had given them fits. The remote detonator had been sticky, but David finally convinced it to explode by switching the frequency. Milton smiled grimly. Roy's black ops group were good men. He'd done a great job picking them in the first place, training them, and honing them into a force to be reckoned with. They were intensely loyal—both to Roy and the CIA.

He made for the tree line and faded from trunk to trunk, moving toward the women. Before he arrived where they were supposed to be, Honor and Glory nearly mowed him down. *"Where's everyone else?"* he asked, determined to fine-tune his telepathic communications, so he didn't sound like he was shouting from the bottom of a well.

Glory ignored his question. *"Roy. Is Roy all right?"*

Milton grabbed her shoulders and shook her. *"Get hold of yourself. He's fine. Where is the rest of your team?"* He considered a terse lecture about answering a superior officer immediately, but bit back the words.

Honor sent a series of images. At least she was trying to avoid anything that could give their position away, even though he didn't believe many of the freaks could possibly be alive after all the pounds of plastique they'd run through.

Once the series of grisly sendings slowed, he said. *"So they knew we were coming, and Charity deserted."*

Honor grimaced, probably at his last word and mouthed, "I'm sorry."

"I know you are." Milton considered Honor's information. Roy and his men should be sifting through the wreckage right about now, and— *Shit!* He keyed his mic and hissed. "Extreme caution. Mission compromised."

Static crackled, and Roy breathed one word, "Glory?"

"With me."

To his credit, Roy didn't ask anything else.

Milton eyed Honor and Glory. "Normally, I'd issue orders, but you have a better feel for your people than I do. What's your pleasure, ladies?"

"If we have a choice," Honor said, her voice cracking with emotion, "we have to hunt for Faith and Hope."

"Not Charity?" He quirked a brow.

"If she doesn't want us to find her, we never will," Glory snapped. "Let's go."

Milton nodded sharply. "Fan out behind me. Once we get close to the building, we'll risk locating their energy."

"Boss." Roy's voice came through his communicator. "Lots of rubble, but no bodies."

"Which means the freaks are probably nearby with unpleasant surprises in store. Fall back. Meet at C point."

Milton turned to Honor and Glory. "We have five minutes to get this done," he said. "Maximize them."

He ran hard for the back of the building, enjoying the enhanced speed and agility the injections conferred. It was as if he'd dropped many years; his body performed like it did back when he was a teenage sniper in the Vietnamese jungles. Lithe, nimble, fast.

A short, hard blast of something flared from Honor, and she switched direction, running so fast her legs blurred.

So much for fan out behind me.

Milton raced after her, sweeping his gaze from side to side, rifle at the ready. The air thickened with the characteristic burnt smell of plastique and particles from the wreckage of the compound. A muted cry burst from Glory, and she passed him too, pelting toward the thick cloud of debris surrounding what had once been the compound. The building had been mostly stone and concrete, and it made a hell of a mess when it exploded. Much worse than wooden timbers would have.

Where two women disappeared into the opaque cloud surrounding the building's perimeter, three emerged with a fourth in Honor's arms, cradled against her body. He sprinted to them and said, "I'll take her."

"Thank you." Hope's voice cracked. "Any minute I was expecting a bullet in my back, or for one of them to blow my mind to smithereens." She drew in one shuddering breath, followed by another and leaned on Glory.

Honor clearly didn't want to let go, but she shifted the other woman into his arms. Faith was breathing, but unconscious. From the angle of her lower legs, he bet they were broken. He wanted to know what happened, but that could wait.

"Can the helicopter come closer?" Honor's question was low, urgent.

"Yes, but we can make our way back to it. She's not that heavy—"

Glory cut him off with a look. "Charity's in my mind. She says we have to leave. Now. She'll hold them off for as long as she can, but she's running out of tricks." Fine lines radiated outward from around her eyes, and pain cut deep around her mouth.

"We didn't kill any of those bastards, did we?" Milton asked.

"Only the six Glory and I shot," Honor's mouth twisted in something that might have been regret.

"Is there any way to extract Charity?" Milton looked from woman to woman.

"She's giving up her life for us." The words tore out of Honor. "If we try to get her out of here, we'll be throwing that sacrifice away."

"How do you know?" Milton persisted. Leaving anyone behind for the wolves wasn't his style.

"Because she's screaming in my head too," Glory said.

"Screaming what?" Milton wanted to shake answers out of the women.

"They've got her in an underground chamber, and they've set her up as bait, expecting we'll return for her," Honor gritted through clenched teeth.

"Maybe if we had more people…" Hope's words trailed off, and her shoulders slumped.

Milton keyed his communicator and herded the women back into the trees. It felt safer there, but probably wasn't since the freaks didn't need a visual. They could track energy signatures. He kept them moving as he keyed the mic again. Faith struggled weakly in his arms.

"You rang, boss?" Roy's flip tone was welcome.

"Position."

Roy rattled off coordinates.

"Stay put. We'll join you. Call the bird. We need to evacuate now."

"No place for it to land here."

Milton had known that was likely. "They'll have to drop a line."

"If things are as bad as I suspect, the boys and I'll hunt in the immediate area for a possible landing pad. We'd be sitting ducks hanging from a rope or a basket."

"Radio me."

Honor grabbed his arm, keyed her own mic, and snapped, "Code," into her communicator.

Milton nodded approvingly and made a chopping motion with one hand. No more talk. He wanted to search the forest with his enhanced senses, but didn't want to tip the freaks off about their location any more than he already had.

They traveled in silence. He followed the GPS strapped to his wrist. The women had their own internal compass mechanisms. Maybe he did too, but now wasn't the time to try something unfamiliar. Faith squirmed against him and moaned softly. *"Ssht. You're safe,"* he murmured into her mind.

Her eyes flickered open. They'd shaded to a deep, moss green. She had to be in major pain, but she clenched her teeth together and gave him a weak thumbs-up sign. Good. He didn't want to stop, fish the morphine out of his field kit, and inject her, but he would if he had to.

Minutes passed as he made his way over obstacles and through thick undergrowth. He split his attention, alert for any alteration in the status quo that might signal they were under attack. He didn't think his mind was vulnerable to the freaks, courtesy of the injections, but it might be. Just in case, he shielded himself like Glory taught him, wishing to hell he knew more about exactly what his newly conferred skills could do. An immediate benefit was night vision as clear as if he wore specialized goggles. Given how dark the night was, and how rugged the terrain, being able to see obstacles before he stumbled over them—especially with Faith in his arms— was a huge plus.

Milton pushed forward. Roy and his men had spent the last

weeks honing their augmented bodies and minds. Milton joined them for a few sessions, but certainly not the majority of them. It was an oversight he planned to correct as soon as he got a chance.

He refocused. They had to get out of here before he could do anything. Diverting even the smallest amount of energy away from the task at hand was a very bad idea.

His communicator beeped, followed by a string of numbers. He decoded the coordinates, grateful for the eidetic memory he'd had even before the injections, and fed the course correction into his GPS. He stopped moving long enough to make certain Hope, Honor, and Glory knew where they were headed before picking up his pace again.

The fine hairs on the back of his neck felt odd, and his stomach coiled into a tight knot of apprehension. He'd learned to trust his instincts in the jungles of Southeast Asia, and he trusted them now. Their message was clear. Someone was waiting for them, and the trap was close to springing shut. Since altering their course was out of the question—not with one of them badly injured—speed was their only option.

He glanced at the GPS. Five minutes to Roy's location. Maybe a little more. It was a miracle he found a spot for the bird to touch down in this welter of fallen timber, overgrown forest, and thick underbrush.

"Freeze!" Glory shouted in frantic-sounding telepathy.

Honor plastered herself over the front of his body, shielding the helpless woman in his arms. Glory and Hope shouldered their assault rifles, facing in opposite directions.

He heard the characteristic beep of a timer counting down just before the forest dissolved in a moving mass of greenery. He dropped to the ground—safer there—and tucked Faith into a hollow, sheltering her with his body. The transition must've forced the broken ends of the bones in her legs against each other, but her screams of pain were obliterated by a series of explosions that battered his senses.

Where was the epicenter? Had the freaks blown up the chopper, or was it still in the air?

Milton lifted his head. Honor was right next to him. Glory and Hope were five feet away. All three met his gaze and nodded gravely. Trees cracked around them, buckling in residual shock waves as they crashed against one another. The chopper may as well be five miles away, for all the good it would do them now. If the forest floor had been hard to navigate before, it would be impossible until trees stopped falling.

"Boss?" Roy's crisp voice, devoid of flippancy this time, was welcome.

"Still here. All of us. The bird?"

"Tree fell on it. Still assessing the damage. I think she'll fly if we can move a few things around."

Milton did some lightning-fast mental calculations. "I'll call in another, but first I'll activate our fighter escort. Things will get noisy, but maybe it'll discourage those bastards from setting off any more charges."

"Ten four." Roy disconnected.

Milton motioned to the women. "See that place where the oak was uprooted. We're going to take advantage of the root hole to ride this next part out."

"I'll get Faith," Honor placed her arms under the other woman. "Do what you have to."

Glory and Hope helped, and the three half belly-crawled, half crab-walked, to where he'd indicated. Fallen trees above the root hole created a natural protection, so it was as good a place as any to wait things out.

He keyed his mike in the pattern that would alert their fighter jet escort, followed by two sets of coded coordinates: his and Roy's. If they got extremely lucky, the carnage would miss them. Made sense. The freaks wouldn't want to be anywhere near the unstable forest, so they were probably holed up some distance away. Otherwise, why use bombs on timers? If they were close, they wouldn't have needed them.

Minutes dribbled by. Milton moved next to the women, but remained edgily alert until the pilot in the lead jet said, "Got a bead on 'em, boss. Heat signature from a bunch of bodies packed like sardines in a tin. Sit tight. Shouldn't be too bad, since they're over a mile from your location."

Milton shucked his field pack and dug for the comprehensive medical kit he always carried.

"What are you doing?" Honor asked. Her voice cracked, and she removed her own pack to get a water bottle.

"We're going to stabilize Faith's legs, and I'm going to give her something for pain."

"If you get the bones positioned right," Faith spoke for the first time, "I'll work on healing myself."

Glory patted her hand. "You do that. We'll get you out of here."

The other woman cracked a pain-riddled grin. "Never doubted it for a moment."

Milton dropped a morphine ampule into a stainless steel field syringe, screwed on a needle, and plunged it into Faith's thigh, through her fatigues. Booming sounded to the northwest that got progressively louder until the ground shook beneath them. More tree parts rained down.

"Will it get any closer?" Honor asked.

Milton shook his head. "Shouldn't. Want to tell me what happened with Charity?"

"Not particularly," Glory muttered.

"Let me rephrase that." Milton gave a quick, hard jerk on Faith's leg to align the bones.

She bit off a muffled yelp, and ground out, "Thanks."

"One of you will tell me what happened with Charity. Now." He repeated the procedure on Faith's other leg, before wrapping both her lower limbs in stout Ace wraps from the knees down.

Glory and Honor exchanged a look. He thought it likely they

were communicating privately. Even though it grated, he gave them space. He'd already ordered them to talk. More orders wouldn't hurry things up.

Honor resettled one of Faith's legs and twitched the wrap into tighter folds. "Charity didn't follow us into the building. Glory and I considered scrapping the mission and going after her—"

"But we didn't," Glory cut in. "It would've been a huge protocol breach."

Milton finished with Faith and repackaged his field kit, stuffing everything back into his rucksack. "You still haven't told me what she did," he prodded as he resettled the body harness around his shoulders.

"Found the Nameless Ones," Honor gritted out. "Told them enough to make them trust she had information, wanted back into the fold, and was willing to share her knowledge for sanctuary."

"And you know this how?" Milton furled his brows.

"She's been feeding us information. Not often, and nothing for the past half hour."

Milton sucked air past his teeth. "I'm surprised they believed her."

"Charity can be pretty convincing when she wants something," Honor said. Her voice was devoid of inflection, but Milton flashed back to Charity barreling into his office and throwing herself into his arms.

"Go on," he barked.

"She must've fed them just enough truth mixed in with fabrication to string them along," Honor murmured.

"Yeah." Glory jumped in. "I'm pretty sure they used their own veracity indicators to test whatever came out of her mouth."

"Once she got close to as many Nameless Ones as she thought she was likely to, she channeled her mental ability to kill them." Honor twisted her hands in her lap. "According to her, she knocked out twenty-five, but she always was prone to exaggeration."

Milton frowned. "So why couldn't she escape after that?"

"Because they're all linked." Faith spoke up from where she lay on the ground. "They threw her into one of the isolation cells that was still more or less intact after you got done bombing the compound. Some of them were torturing her for information, while others set up a perimeter to snag us when we came back for her."

"We assume Charity took her remaining power—which couldn't have been much—and warded herself. That was when she warned us we had to get out now," Honor said.

"Did they kill her?" Milton persisted, needing to know.

Honor hesitated. "She wasn't dead when I last sensed her in that iso cell, but there are too many residual shockwaves in the air right now for me to tell anything."

"She'd almost have to be dead," Glory said, "unless the airstrike interrupted whatever the freaks were doing to her."

"She was on her way out—or she thought she was—when she told us to get moving." Hope narrowed her eyes. "That was right before the trees turned into tinker toys."

"Christ! She was a regular latter day martyr," Milton said.

"She didn't plan to be," Glory retorted. "She was certain she could outthink them and get herself out once she'd done maximum damage."

"How could you possibly know that?" Milton asked.

"Because we knew her as well as anyone," Honor said. "Charity was a lot of things. And maybe not very stable because of her genetics, but she wasn't into heroics."

"Maybe you didn't know her as well as you thought," Milton said as he chewed through the information. "What she did—taking on an entire compound full of freaks by herself—is as heroic an act as I've witnessed in all the years I've done this."

"Except she didn't look at them as freaks," Hope said quietly. "Up until recently, we were part of them, no matter how we felt about it."

His communicator crackled, and he listened intently before turning to the women. "You likely heard that," he said, "but the men freed the chopper. It's not so damaged it won't fly. In a few minutes, it'll hover, and you'll load."

"What about you?" Honor sent a significant glance his way, obviously having read between the lines of his carefully crafted words.

"I'm going after Charity. We don't know for sure that she's dead. I've never abandoned a man in the field unless I absolutely had to. I'm not going to start now. My first guess is the freaks made a run for the secondary location my pilots ferreted out after we blew it up. Makes sense they'd want to see if anyone was left."

"The Nameless Ones would assume they could come back and finish her off whenever they wanted to," Glory murmured.

"It should've occurred to them that we'd risk an airstrike." Milton snorted. "Maybe they don't know how accurately we can pinpoint things like that."

"Regardless of what they know, or don't know, I'm going with you," Honor said. Her back was ramrod straight, and she stared him down, her features carved into a silent challenge.

He started to tell her no, that he'd be faster and safer on his own, but something in her eyes—a fierce, determined gleam—stopped him. He tried to tell himself that was all there was, that working with her by his side was secondary.

But he didn't quite believe it.

CHAPTER 8

*H*onor blew out a tense breath as the metal cage containing Faith disappeared into the belly of the chopper, and the door slid shut. Everyone except her and Milton were already aboard, and the helicopter canted as it gained speed and elevation, whirring its way back to the safety of the CIA compound at Langley.

"Will it come back for us?" She brushed a hand across her face. Judging from how dirty her fingers were, she left grimy streaks in their wake.

"No. I've ordered up another. Plus Langley's sending a car."

"Why both?"

"Always good to have backup." He handed her the rifle she'd leaned against a tree, and she draped the strap across her body.

Even though it had come in handy inside the compound, it was heavy and clunky. A long way from feeling like a part of her, which made the gun easy to forget. She winced. Not very soldier-like. She'd need to do better.

Grateful Milton hadn't chided her for sloppiness, Honor dialed in her enhanced senses and pointed. "She's that way."

"Can you tell if she's still alive?"

"You already asked that."

"I know. We'll plan something different if we're extricating a corpse."

Honor cocked her head to one side, confused. "There'd be no point in going after her if she was dead."

"There's always a point." Milton smiled grimly. "If I was dead, the last place I'd want my carcass is stuck behind enemy lines."

"I think she's alive. I'm pretty sure I sense her, but I'm not willing to risk a bigger jolt of energy until we're clear of all this debris." Honor clambered over a pile of broken tree trunks. Letting herself down on the far side, she was confronted with more piles stretching in every direction. "Christ! This is going to take a long time."

He came up behind her. "Maybe not so long as all that. Can you climb trees?"

"Sure." Honor looked up. "I never have, but how hard could it be?"

"Have you ever slacklined or ziplined?"

"No, but I understand the concept. Maybe ziplining would be better. I'm not sure my balance is good enough to walk a tightrope."

Milton didn't answer, just picked the biggest tree still standing in the area and clambered up it as if he had cleats attached to his hands and feet.

Honor followed at a more sedate pace. By the time her head was even with his feet, he'd lassoed a neighboring tree and was pulling the line taught.

"Work your way up and around me," he instructed. "Secure your rifle across your back first, so it's not bouncing. I heard the stock hit the tree as you climbed up to me."

She balanced on a good-sized branch. It swayed, and she tightened the rifle's straps until the gun hugged her back before making her way to Milton's side. He draped webbing around her hips, snugging it as he moved it into place, and then hooked it to the line above them. "Momentum won't get you there," he cautioned. "Use your hands on the line to pull yourself along. Move as fast as you can."

Honor nodded and swung her body over the forty foot drop. It looked like a long way down, so she focused on the line above her head. She swung her body in an arc until her fingertips brushed the line. Once she had it, she pulled herself to the next tree and wrapped her legs around a stout branch. Certain she was stable, she unhooked and pushed the webbing back into the space between them.

For long moments, the webbing and clip hung suspended. Milton jerked the line hard. Once. Twice. The third tug sent the webbing skittering back his way. He clipped in and made his way to her. "Now comes the tricky part." He twitched the line, and it unwound from the far tree.

Honor stared as he reeled it in. "That was barely attached," she said, her throat dry.

"It was good enough to hold both of us."

"But—"

"No buts." He lassoed another tree and set them up to do the same thing again. "It's an old rappel trick. If climbers had to carry a different rope for every single move, they'd be so burdened, they'd never be able to maneuver. So they arrange things to retrieve their ropes."

"Does it always work?"

"No."

Honor didn't trust herself to say anything nice, so she clamped her jaws shut. After five more aerial tram tricks, she climbed down a large fir tree and settled her feet on the ground. Actually, the ziplining, or slacklining or whatever they'd done, had been damned smooth. Inspired. They'd hopscotched through the worst of the chopped up forest in less than half an hour. If they'd been stuck on the ground, it would've taken far longer.

Milton dropped to her side and draped the coiled line across one shoulder, looping his arm through it. "Got to get you gals some parachute practice."

"Probably easy compared with what we just did. You've had years to hone commando skills. The Nameless Ones taught us basic combat maneuvers, but they're not the same."

"No," he agreed, "they're not. Have you checked on Charity in the last few minutes?"

"Just did. And I'm more convinced than I was earlier that she's alive, but she's not answering me."

"Why to both?"

"Her energy's too strong for her to be dead. About the other, she could be unconscious, or so pissed off I'm still here, she's not bothering to answer me."

"Since you have the link to her, lead out."

Honor started forward, but stopped abruptly.

"What is it?" Milton drew next to her.

"I sense more than just her."

His service sidearm materialized in his hand so quickly, she never saw him draw it. "That's a lot bigger than my 9mm," she observed.

"Better stopping power. It's a semiautomatic Smith and Wesson 45. What do you feel out there? I just sent my senses outward, but what comes back feels like gibberish."

Honor held out her hand. "Link to me. See the world the way I do."

Milton grasped her hand. His grip was warm and sure, and she never wanted to let go. Instead, she let her long-range sensitivity flow into him. Once they were joined, she cast her consciousness in a large net and stopped each place she sensed something alive. "This one is probably a bear," she said. "And that one's something small, maybe a group of raccoons or foxes."

"Keep going." He tightened his hold on her.

"This is from a normal human. So's this. Charity's right here, but I sense two more life forms beyond her. Freaks." She stumbled over the word, told herself she was being too sensitive, and moved on.

"So four in all, plus Charity?" At her nod, he went on. "I sense the difference between animal energies and humanoid. Not so much between non-augmented humans and freaks. How can you tell which one is Charity?"

Honor moved her attention from the last normal human she'd sensed back to Charity. "If you ever played a musical instrument, you looked for patterns. It's what I look for. We, the genetically modified, have a certain pattern to how our energy pings back. You have another. It's not all that subtle, maybe the difference between a waltz and modern dance."

"Let me feel it again." Milton dragged their combined energy from where she'd identified Charity to another of the energy fountains. "It's not that different," he said.

"It is, once you're tuned into it. The energy moves faster for our females than our males. And it moves slower for purely humans." Honor took a deep breath. "I hate to burn up any more time, but this is as good an opportunity as you're likely to get to notice the differences."

She moved her focus to one of the normal humans, then to Charity, then to what she assumed had to be two Nameless Ones.

"This will take practice," Milton muttered.

Honor snorted. "Yeah, like the whole gun thing for me. I'm not worried about the garden-variety humans I sensed, but we will run into a couple Nameless Ones. Maybe they were left behind to ride herd on Charity."

"Have you tried talking to her again?"

"Yeah." Honor shook her head. "No dice."

Milton tapped something into his wrist-mounted computer, apparently got a response, and typed something else.

"What?" She realized her hand was still gripped in his and pulled free. Her hand felt cold without his fingers curled around it.

"The second bird's here. I told it to hover over our objective."

Honor squared her shoulders. "May as well get this over with. Don't trust the men. If they're alive and kicking, we'll have to kill them."

"Without an offer of amnesty?" Milton sent a strange look her way.

"Depends what they did to Charity." Honor sprinted forward, not wanting to continue a conversation that made her look vindictive.

What was left of the compound came into view. She got her bearings and headed for where she knew the iso cells were. Because four of the cells were underground, and the building was pretty much reduced to rubble, she deduced Charity had to be in one of the subterranean holding pens. Getting to her might require digging.

Honor fanned out energy, hunting for the Nameless Ones she'd sensed. They saved her the trouble of locating them by sprinting from the ruins.

"Hold it right there." Milton's voice boomed from behind her, and she heard the metallic click of the safety releasing on his semi-automatic pistol.

As an afterthought, she unslung her rifle and balanced the stock against her shoulder, pointing at the men. "Where's Charity?" she demanded.

"That bitch is crazier than a rabid dog." One of the men grunted.

"We tried to keep her up here with us, but she bit and scratched and kept trying to kill us with her mind, so we had to lock her up," the other man said. His amber animal-like eyes held vertical slit pupils, just like all the genetically modified men. Black hair hung straight to his shoulders. Both men wore black trousers, black T-shirts, and camo jackets. Tall, lace-up field boots covered their lower calves.

"Are there normal humans in the wreckage?" Milton asked.

The Nameless Ones exchanged a pointed look. "Not sure how

you'd know about them unless she…" One hooked a thumb at Honor. "…told you."

"What are they doing here?" Honor asked.

"We're geneticists. We've been working on perfecting V4," one of the men replied.

"So? I don't understand the connection," Honor pressed.

"We needed additional genes," the other man said. "For that we needed humans."

"You kidnapped them?" Milton sounded like he was ready to kill something.

"In a manner of speaking," the first man said and shook his head. "How the hell do you suppose your human geneticists and biochemists got the raw materials to create us to begin with?"

"They used their own cells," Milton answered as if he were in a classroom reciting a well-worn truism.

"That's what they told you." Honor kept her voice quiet. "In the same spirit that they never bothered mentioning they scrapped V1 and V2 in a wholesale slaughter."

"Are you telling me the human scientists—leaders in genetic research and biochemistry—kept human beings locked away to borrow their genetic material?" Milton's voice rose.

"It's exactly what she's telling you." The slightly taller of the Nameless Ones stepped forward. "If you don't believe us, the humans you sensed are two of those scientists. We could drum the truth out of them—once we let them wake up."

"What do you mean wake up? Why would they be asleep? You're talking in riddles." Milton shut his mouth so hard, Honor heard his teeth clack together.

"We've kept them in a permanent state of suspended animation —for years. It's easier than listening to them argue about why we should let them go."

"Fuck." Milton scrubbed a hand through his hair. "I'm starting to think it was a good thing we never found any of the scientists."

"They'd have kept right on lying to you," Honor said. "I may hate the Nameless Ones, but the scientists are a part of history all of us learned."

"Before we get too far off track, we're requesting amnesty. It was advertised over the Internet," one of the Nameless Ones said. "I'm Frank. My fellow genetic researcher is Tony." He gestured toward the other man.

Tony stepped to Frank's side. "We saw the announcement come through, but neither of us could figure out how to get out of here to take advantage of it."

"Keep an eye on them," Honor said to Milton and moved to a rubble pile where she tossed blocks aside.

"If you're after the other woman," Frank said. "We'll get her for you. It's a mess down there."

"Hit something wrong," Tony put in, "and the whole shebang is likely to fall on your head. It's going to be a trick and a half getting the crazy one out if she's flailing like she was on the trip in."

"Which is why you should take me," Honor said. "She knows me."

"I don't want you going anywhere with him." Milton trotted to her side, his gun still deployed.

"For fuck's sake, stop negotiating and get me out of here," Charity screamed.

Honor's head snapped back, her auditory cortex ringing. Annoyance vied with relief that Charity was very much alive. *"Nice something got your attention."* Honor cut it off there. No reason to antagonize her unstable friend. *"Do you promise to behave if one of the men escorts you?"*

"I'll promise anything. Just. Get. Me. Out."

"We heard that," Frank said. He looked around, opened his mouth, and appeared to think better of whatever he wanted to say.

"I'm on it." Tony disappeared down a hole in the ground.

Frank moved closer to Honor and pitched his voice low. "She's one of the unstable configurations. We've had some luck replotting their genetic arrangement."

"What happens if you don't?" Honor whispered back.

"The inevitable. They sink into madness and have to be culled."

Because talking about Charity as if she were an animal in need of euthanasia was disconcerting, Honor switched gears. "About the scientists. Are they in any kind of shape to transport?"

"Depends how their pods stood up to the bombs and earthquakes that followed."

"We need to bring them with us," Milton concurred. "Once they come around, they could be a rich source of data."

"Maybe," Frank said.

"What do you mean?" Milton's voice was laced with suspicion. "What did you do to them?"

"It's more what they did to themselves," Frank said. "Experimenting on your own kind takes a particular toll. And we've kept them asleep for most of the last seven years. They're probably not much of a step up from vegetables at this point—even if they do regain consciousness."

Charity limped through the hole in the ground with Tony right behind her. Honor rushed to her side and held out her arms. "You were really brave."

Charity curled her upper lip. "Can it. You were pretty steamed when I didn't join you and Glory. Don't pretend different now."

"Can't I be glad to see you?" Pain for her friend filled her, twisting her insides into a knot of discomfort.

"No. I don't deserve it." Charity turned away.

"Do you want to come back to Langley?" Honor asked, recalling their earlier conversation. "You're not a prisoner. If you're done with us, I'm certain Milton will see you're set up anywhere you want to live."

Tony walked toward Charity, but not too close. "We can help you," he said.

"How? What *help* could possibly come from a Nameless One?"

"No guarantees," Frank cut in, "but we might be able to keep your DNA configuration from eroding further. Living like you do can't be comfortable."

"Especially knowing what the future holds," Tony added. "And the hallucinations and delusions must be scary as hell."

"Why do you think I put myself square in the middle of a suicide mission?" Charity demanded, hands on her hips and madness dancing deep in her eyes. "I'm not good for anything else."

"You could be." Honor tried to go to Charity, but the other woman turned away from her.

"Maybe I don't want to be."

Milton joined Honor. "Tell us what you want, Charity, and I'll try to make it happen for you."

Shrieks of crazed laughter yielded to huge sobs that shook Charity until she trembled. Honor gathered her close and crooned wordlessly, gratified when the other woman clung to her.

Charity finally quieted enough to pull away. "Why are you being kind to me? After I threw myself at your boyfriend?"

"First I've heard about it, and he's not my boyfriend." Honor smiled softly. "At least not yet. You and the other women, well you're the only family I have. We've got to watch out for each other. If we don't, then who will?"

"Good point." Charity took a step backward and wiped her damp cheeks. She turned to face Milton. "I guess I'll go back to Langley. Maybe the boys here..." She waved a hand toward Frank and Tony. "...can fix me."

Tony glanced at Milton. "How much space will I have to bring things?"

"How much do you need?"

"Once the others find out Frank and I defected, we'll be targeted. I'll never be able to return to any compound, so there are some scientific supplies I'd like to bring along."

"Things you couldn't get from normal lab supply houses?" Milton furled his brows.

Tony nodded. "Yes. We've got the pods with the scientists too."

"If you want them," Frank broke in. "We wouldn't mind leaving—"

Tony elbowed him, and the rest of his thought died unspoken.

Milton tapped a few more keys on his wrist computer. "Two ambulances are on their way for the scientists. We should be able to take the rest of whatever you want to bring with you between the helicopter and the car I requested earlier."

Honor wound her arm around Charity's waist. "I meant what I said about you being brave."

Fresh tears welled. "Thanks, hon. That's the nicest thing anyone's ever said to me."

"You'd do the same for me. When you get down to it, you just did."

Surprise flickered in Charity's green eyes. "You're right. I was so focused on finding an honorable way out, I wasn't thinking about it that way."

"Hate to break up this love-fest, but you're not going anywhere." A Nameless One raced into the clearing, followed by two others.

Frank eyed them with a sour expression. "Spying on us, were you?"

"Let's just say we thought it odd you were so keen on providing nanny services for the crazy bitch. We'd have killed her, but—"

Charity bared her teeth and hissed at him. "Back off, you fucking bastard."

"You're the one who needs to back off, bitch," another newcomer snarled. "We hate to murder our own, but we do what we have to."

"Like hell you hate to *murder your own*," Honor faced off against them and snarled. "What about the women I found dead in this compound?"

The air around Frank and Tony shifted until it swirled in transcendent waves. Power poured from them, and the three Nameless Ones dropped to the ground, clawing at their throats.

"Keep it flowing," Frank ground out, "until they're dead."

A slow horror filled Honor as she watched the men writhing in the dirt. Her kind had degenerated to a point she'd never imagined in her worst nightmares. Turning on one another like beasts. Maybe none of them deserved to live.

Tony spared a glance at Milton. "I'd hustle those transports along. We've got to get out of here."

"You can quit," Frank told Tony and dropped his hands. He was breathing hard and his mouth was set in a harsh line.

Tony walked forward and toed one of the fresh corpses. "Maybe we can quit for the moment," he said, his voice deadly quiet, "but we just took a stand. One we'll never see the end of, no matter how much we want to."

Honor watched the exchange and for the first time ever felt a flicker of compassion for a Nameless One.

CHAPTER 9

Milton stepped into the backseat of the dusty, black SUV, following Honor's high, tight backside. His fingers itched to pat her ass, but he restrained himself. She'd laugh it off—maybe—but it felt disrespectful. Surely she knew what a great ass she had. She didn't need him to point it out.

The driver got in, slammed his door, and the SUV rolled down a rutted dirt road on its way to pavement. His navy windbreaker was emblazoned with the CIA logo, and his brown hair was cut close to his scalp. "You were ready to roll, sir?" A pair of shrewd gray eyes met Milton's in the rearview mirror.

"More than ready," Milton confirmed, "but next time ask first."

"You got it, sir." The driver focused on the road ahead again.

Charity, Frank, and Tony had left with the second chopper. Roy and his team were long since back at Langley, along with Glory, Hope, and Faith. Scientific materials and computer drives were spread between the ambulances, the helicopter, and their car. Neither of the scientists had made it. Their pods were crushed under tons of earth. It hadn't been possible to get close enough to them to even consider CPR, let alone dig out their remains.

"What a lost opportunity," Milton murmured.

"The scientists?" Honor asked. When he nodded, she went on, "Maybe you don't want to know what you might've learned from them."

"If Tony and Frank are telling the truth, maybe not, but there are some huge credibility gaps between what I thought was going on at those breeding farms and the reality. Fuck! It's almost like a resurrection of Nazi Germany and their human gene manipulation experiments."

"There are similarities." She leaned her head against the seat back and shut her eyes.

"Tired?" he asked solicitously.

"I passed *tired* hours ago." She smiled, but it looked forced. "I'm running on fumes, wisps. Probably don't have enough energy left to light a match. When I blow through bunches of power, I need time to recharge."

"I didn't expect this operation to be easy," he said, "but there were considerably more twists and turns than I anticipated." He hesitated. "I'm sorry we got there too late to save the women."

"Yeah. Me too. To be honest, I haven't been able to get them out of my head."

"We learned a few things."

Like what?" She turned a quizzical expression his way.

"Apparently we still have a leak. I thought I found all the Nameless Ones who'd infiltrated Langley, but I was wrong."

"Not necessarily." She chewed on her lower lip. "The women's bodies were still warm when we got to them. It looked as if they'd been gunned down execution style in their beds. Hope and Faith found the same thing, but they actually interrupted Nameless Ones killing the last few. It's how Faith's legs got broken. One of the men clubbed her. If Hope hadn't killed him, she and Faith never would've gotten away."

He'd wondered what had happened. "Why wouldn't the women have struggled? Fought? Done something? They must've been jolted awake after the first gunshot."

"Yeah, Glory and I talked about that a little. The Nameless Ones have a form of mass hypnosis they can employ. Our best guess was they immobilized the women, so they couldn't fight back."

White hot anger scoured his insides, making them burn. "That's so appalling, I almost can't imagine it. Puts the Nameless Ones right up there with the Vietcong."

"How so?"

"They bombed their own villages to keep us from rescuing any of them who might've changed sides." He curled his lips derisively. "Better dead than free."

"How old were you when you fought in Southeast Asia?"

The question surprised him. "Not very. Why?"

The smile she sent his way was laced with compassion. "No special reason. It seems like it made a big impression on you, so I figured you couldn't have been very old."

"It shaped a lot of who I am." His words came slowly. "Made it hard to trust anyone. I spent years in the military after Nam, but none of it had quite the same impact."

"I never fought the same way you have, but I still know what you mean." Honor touched his hand briefly and then reached up and started unbraiding her hair. When the braids were mostly undone, she threaded her fingers into her hair and rubbed her scalp. "What time is it anyway?" She glanced out the window. "Noon? Afternoon?"

"Your second guess is closer."

"It'll be night by the time we get back, huh?" She slumped against her seat.

"It'll be dark before we hit the Interstate," he said. "You can catch a nap."

"Do we get dinner?"

"Sure. If you want some. You call it, Honor. Would you rather sleep or eat?"

She grinned. "It's a hard choice, but maybe I can do a little of both. How far until we get to a town?"

"Maybe an hour. It's not far, but the roads aren't that great."

"Wake me at the first burger stand."

Her eyelids shut almost before she was done talking. Milton watched her slide deeper into sleep. Her eyes twitched beneath her closed lids, and her lips parted slightly. He remembered how those lips felt beneath his, and he longed to trace their line with his fingertips. Even sunk into exhaustion, she was lovely. Dark hair with just a hint of curl to it framed her striking, runway-model features.

As her face relaxed into sleep, its stark lines softened. Her forehead was high, her dark brows cutting across it at an angle. A fine sprinkling of freckles scattered across her sculpted cheekbones. He'd never noticed them before, but the dirt and grime streaking her face made them stand out. Dark smudges sat beneath her eyes, and her grit-crusted hands splayed across her body where she'd wrapped her arms around herself.

He wondered if she was cold and shucked out of his jacket to drape it gently around her torso. She made a soft noise and leaned toward the jacket's residual warmth, encouraging him to tuck it more firmly around her. He bent toward the driver in the front seat and murmured. "Heat, please."

The field agent nodded and reached for the controls.

Milton slouched against the seat back. It finally felt safe to let his guard down—at least a little. The women had performed well. Despite not being trained operatives, they'd managed to stay alive. While he'd have been more comfortable with them following his every order exactly, he understood it sometimes wasn't possible. If Honor and Glory had chosen to go after Charity, both teams would've lost even the small advantage they had and likely been blown to Hell and back before they had a chance to cripple the compound.

His thoughts turned to Frank and Tony, if those were their real names. Not that it mattered. The women had numbers until they'd named themselves, and none of the freaks held any kind of identification like drivers' licenses or social security cards. It worried him a little that they were in the helicopter, but he trusted Roy and his men to keep a close eye on things. Besides, the men had killed their own, slamming any return doors in their faces. Obviously the offer of amnesty hadn't gotten nearly as wide a coverage in the compounds as he'd hoped it would. It was a good bet Frank and Tony weren't the only ones who wanted out—in addition to the women.

If the Nameless Ones were going to murder the women, he'd have to come up with a better strategy. One that gave them no warning at all, or better yet, one that would cripple their ability to do something like they'd masterminded last night. He thought about the mass hypnosis Honor mentioned. Could the women pull something like that off before they hit the next compound?

He didn't remember falling asleep, but the jolt of the car moving from rutted dirt to pavement woke him. Honor leaned against him, and he'd draped an arm around her at some point, cradling her next to his body. She sighed and pushed closer to him, still deeply asleep from the sound of her breathing.

No matter how awkward things are when we're awake, we can take comfort from one another while we're sleeping.

The thought warmed him. So did the woman drowsing at his side.

Five years had passed since his last marriage went up in smoke. He supposed he could've tried harder, but the plain truth was he didn't want to. Drawn by Maggie's showgirl beauty, he hadn't looked much deeper than a ready source of sex. He'd ignored her Daddy-complex and a need to be taken care of that bordered on the pathological. Breath hissed between his teeth. Those few months were far from his proudest moments. It had been a relief when she'd found a more likely prospect, and he'd come home to a mercifully empty house after a protracted trip to the U.K.

The divorce had been short, sweet, and expensive.

Guilt money; he'd paid her for her trouble.

He wondered if she ever gave him another thought and hoped to hell she didn't. A slight sensation rippled through his forehead; he reached to scratch what he assumed was some errant bug, but didn't find anything.

Honor shifted and straightened, moving away from him.

When he looked at her, her green eyes were open and focused on him. "Charity dug up your marriages," she said without preamble, "and warned me you weren't good boyfriend material."

Puzzle pieces clattered into a whole. "You were in my head just now. That strange feeling was you."

Honor nodded. "Didn't mean to be, but sometimes it just happens." She shrugged. "I'd apologize, except I'm not sorry. I want to know more about you."

Pleasure took root inside him, but caution ran deeper. "How'd Charity find out anything about me?" he growled.

"How do you think?" she countered. "By going where she shouldn't have."

He should've felt angry, violated. Instead a snorting laugh emerged. "It's a whole new ball game with you gals, isn't it? Can't keep you out of any of the databases, and there's not much point in trying. What we need to do is enlist you to help us build better firewalls."

A sheepish grin lit her face. "I figured you'd be livid."

"I should be." He tried to sound stern.

"But you're not."

Milton held out his arms, and she came into them. When she was close, he aimed his words just for her. No way could the driver hear them over the noise of the engine. "I'll tell you anything you want to know about me. Your friends don't have to hack into personnel records."

An uncharacteristic giggle sounded, followed by another. "Charity will be disappointed. She enjoys undercover sleuthing."

"We all do." He tightened his hold on her and stroked his fingers down her back. She wove her arms around him and hugged him in return.

"You feel nice," she murmured. "Even though we're filthy and stinky, you still feel nice."

"You do too." He paused a beat. "I'm still trying to figure out how to get you out from under my command. How would you feel about being assigned to Roy's team?"

She tilted her head back and looked at him. "I'd rather stay with the women." Fine lines cut into her forehead as she thought about the problem. "It makes better sense for us to be together since we augment one another's power."

"I'm open to ideas." He tipped a finger under her chin, holding her gaze. "I want to get to know you—without breaking too many company rules."

"If we had another half dozen women," she said, "then we could form two units."

Since it fed into his thoughts from earlier, he asked, "Is there any possibility you could manipulate the mass hypnosis you told me about to immobilize enough of the Nameless Ones to avoid another massacre like last night's?"

"Yeah. Huh. We'll never get any more women if they keep killing them." She kneaded the tight muscles in his back and shoulders.

It was all he could do not to groan with pleasure at her touch. "You didn't exactly answer me."

"Because I don't know. None of us have ever done that, but maybe Frank and Tony will have some ideas for how to make it work."

"Since you're awake," the driver called from the front seat, "did you want to stop for some chow?"

"Sure," Milton said. "That'd be great. Maybe just a drive through."

"We're not exactly fit company for a real restaurant," Honor concurred.

Milton snorted. "We'd sure clear the place out fast enough."

The driver laughed. "Glad you said it, sir. It's been a bit ripe even up here. How does that Taco Bell look?"

"What do you think?" Milton asked Honor.

"Sounds great! Let's do it."

HONOR WAS glad to see the CIA compound roll into view. It had been dark for a long time, and she wanted to shower off the filth of the last twenty-four hours. Once she was clean, she planned to crawl into bed and set her neural processing unit to sleep mode.

She also wanted the man sitting next to her.

They spent their time in the car cuddling and talking, and the more she found out about Milton, the more she respected him. He was anything but the womanizer Charity feared. Quite the contrary. If anything, he was married to his jobs. First the Marine Corps and then the CIA. He'd retired from the Marines as a Colonel, and the CIA happened as an afterthought, interrupting his plans to kick back, hunting and fishing in northern Montana where he'd been raised. The Pentagon had invited him to take over in an acting capacity, and he did such a stellar job, they talked him into staying.

The next fifteen years passed quickly, especially after he got caught up in the freaks' rebellion seven years before.

"Penny for your thoughts?" He swiped a finger across the side of her mouth. "Taco sauce," he explained in response to her puzzled look.

"I'm surprised something that mundane is even noticeable on top of how much crud I figure is on my face."

He shrugged. "Well, the rest of it's black, and this was red. Made it stick out like a sore thumb."

She laughed.

"Maybe there's a future for you as a field operative after all," he said.

"What do you mean?"

"If you can laugh after the hell we lived through, it bodes well."

A place deep inside her warmed at the unexpected vote of confidence in her ability.

"Sir?" The driver interrupted once they'd gone past the guard station. "Where to?"

"How about if you let us off on the next corner, and we'll figure it out from there," Milton replied.

"You got it." The driver pulled up to a curb and stopped. "Where do you want the rest of the stuff in the back?"

"Biochemistry lab. It's the closest we come to genetics around here."

"I could contact NIH—" the driver began.

Milton cut him off. "Nah. We'll sort all this out later. Once you've unloaded the car, you're off duty for twelve."

"Thank you, sir."

Milton pushed the SUV's door open and got out. His body felt stiff, and he rotated his shoulders. Once Honor joined him, he slammed the door and watched as the car drove slowly away.

"You didn't want him to overhear whatever we decided, huh?" Honor asked.

"It's almost impossible to keep anything secret at Langley." He took her hand. "This is your call, Honor. I'd love to bring you back to my quarters, but it's a pretty big move, and we're both beyond tired."

"Back in the car, you asked about my thoughts. You said something like a penny for them…" Her voice trailed off, as she gathered her courage.

"I did, but we got sidetracked by the taco sauce on your mouth."

"I was thinking about you." The words weren't as hard to say as she feared they'd be. In truth, they rolled off her tongue.

"What exactly were you thinking about me?" he prodded.

"That you're pretty damned amazing."

He tightened his grip on her hand. "Does that mean you want to come home with me?"

"She followed me home, can I keep her?" Honor quipped.

Milton's expression turned serious, his dark eyes lighting with something feral and possessive. "I have a feeling if you come home with me, you'll have God's own time getting shut of me."

"Best offer I've had—ever." Layers of weariness lifted. "Lead out. I wouldn't miss this next part for the world."

CHAPTER 10

Despite her brave words, nervous tension filled Honor as she walked across the darkened campus by Milton's side. His home was at the far edge, separated from other base housing by thick hedges.

"Are you sure about this?" Milton's deep voice rumbled against her ear.

"No. Does it show?"

He stopped walking, turned her to face him, and placed his hands on her shoulders. "You don't have to do this. Not tonight. Not ever. If there's one thing we have, it's time."

"What makes you so certain of that?" She tilted her chin at a defiant angle. "Either one of us might have been killed today."

"But we weren't."

"Still. Nothing is certain." She drew in a slow breath, hunting for a calm center. It wasn't easy with all that maleness a few inches away.

"This is." He angled his head and brought his mouth down on hers. His lips were firm, insistent, and he pushed against hers with his tongue.

Honor opened her mouth and sparred with him. She wrapped

her arms around him and pulled him as close as she could. The smells of dirt, cordite, sweat, and aroused man surrounded her. He slid his hands from her shoulders down her back to her ass, where he cupped the swell of her buttocks.

His cock sprang to life between them, and a hot, slick tongue of flame moved from her belly to between her legs. Breath quickened in her throat, and her nipples hardened into painful buds of need. She sucked on his tongue, still buried in her mouth, as if it was the only thing keeping her on this side of the veil.

Who knew? Maybe it was.

Honor lost track of where he ended and she began. She could stand here forever in the velvety dark lost in a kiss that kept on giving with a life of its own. He bit and suckled her lips, and she bit back. When he ripped his mouth from hers and strung kisses down the side of her neck, she shuddered with wanting him.

"So." He skewered her with his dark gaze, the look she'd seen in the car, alive with wanting her. His voice was low, hungry. "Decide. If we stand out here much longer, I'll drag you behind that stand of trees, and that wasn't how I planned your first time."

"How do you know it'll be my first time?"

"A man knows those things. There's a difference in how virgins feel, but I'll admit I cheated. Two can play the mind harvesting game. Besides you told me earlier."

"What did you have planned for me?" Desire turned her belly into a pool of heat, but she wanted to hear him talk dirty to her.

"Come on." He slipped a hand under her arm and tugged. "That's a conversation for behind closed doors."

Because she couldn't not follow him unless she'd been hogtied, she made her way down a darkened walkway and up several steps to a broad front porch. Milton placed his hand on a sensor that was twin to the ones in many of Langley's buildings, and the door snicked open. He waved his hand over another bank of sensors, and the front room came alive with soft lights.

Honor caught her breath as she looked at the decidedly masculine space. The bookshelf-lined room held dark leather furniture arranged in inviting seating configurations. Oak tables with lamps made from polished wood were set at strategic intervals. A huge television screen took up most of one wall, and a computer desk with a large monitor of its own perched in a corner.

"This is lovely," she said.

"What?" He sent his trademark sardonic grin her way. "You thought I lived in something as sterile as my office?"

Heat that had nothing to do with sex crept from her chest to her neck to her face. "I don't know what I thought," she murmured.

"Actually, I have a horse and cattle ranch in Montana that's truly home. It's been in my family for four generations. I get back there when I can."

"Who takes care of it?"

"A very dedicated group of men." Milton closed the door and passed his palm over another electronic reader to engage the lock.

He gestured toward a door leading from the right side of the living room. "Are you still hungry? Or would you like a drink?"

She glanced at herself. "I think I want a bath before anything. Neither of us smell very good."

"I could pour us drinks, and we could take them into the bathroom with us." He stroked the side of her face with his calloused palm. "A little whiskey would relax you."

"Maybe so." She still felt shaky from their heated kiss outside. "Show me where the bathroom is, and I'll start the shower."

As he spoke he pointed. "Through that door are stairs leading to the second floor. The bathroom's at the far end, and it has a huge tub with Jacuzzi jets. How about if you start filling it? It takes a while."

"Sure." She made her way to the door, feeling his gaze on her, hot and proprietary at the same time. A polished wooden staircase rose in front of her. She could've hunted for a light switch. Instead, she dialed in her night vision and climbed upward. At the top of the stairs, she stopped. The entire second floor was one large room. It held the same comfortable ambience as the lower level. A large bed butted against one wall, with small tables on both sides of it. Mounted on the wall across from the bed was another large screen. At the moment, it was divided into windows, each of which reflected part of Langley's campus. The other side of the room held two beautiful armoires of some kind of dark, shiny wood. A desk took up the remaining corner with a computer and yet one more monitor.

The last thing that caught her eye was a six-foot-tall, glass-fronted cabinet that held a variety of swords and guns, all lovingly mounted in an attractive display.

She made her way to the bathroom, separated from Milton's living area by a bead curtain, and swallowed a gasp. The tub was enormous. It could have held three people, four in a pinch. She knelt and got the water running. Once the temperature was decent, she plugged the drain and took in the rest of the bathroom. Black granite with gold flecks covered the floor. The fixtures were contrasting granite: golden with black veins running through it. The effect was lovely.

"Do you like it?" Milton pushed the clattery beads aside and set two glasses down.

"Is most base housing this…fancy?"

He shook his head. "Nah, but I spend enough time here, I figured I deserve a few creature comforts. I designed this upper floor and footed the bill myself for the improvements I wanted."

She picked up a glass and took a tentative sip. Just as had happened the other night, the liquor burned her mouth and throat, and she gasped for air.

"Swirl it around in your mouth first," he suggested. "It deadens the shock response to the liquor."

When she did as he bade, she found it indeed made the golden liquid easier to swallow. "Those guns and swords out there." She waved a hand. "Have you used all of them?"

"Every single one." He looked pleased with himself. "But we're not going to talk about work. At least not until tomorrow morning."

"I, um, I thought of a problem," she stuttered. "I don't have clean clothes here."

"You can borrow something of mine." He took a step closer. "Any other concerns? Details? Things we need to watch out for?" A teasing light joined the heat in his eyes.

"I can't think of a thing."

"Good." He levered the glass out of her hand and knelt in front of her.

"What are you doing?"

"Unlacing your boots. You're not planning to bathe with them on, are you?"

Honor tossed a frantic glance at the tub. "It's not full enough yet."

"You're scared." His fingers worked the knots out of her boot-laces, and he got her to lean against him while he jockeyed them off her feet. "I've seen you with much less on than this in the practice arena."

He rose to his feet in a single, fluid motion and pulled his top over his head. He'd left the jacket he'd draped around her in the car downstairs.

Honor gaped at his naked chest. Slabs of muscle ran across his shoulders, bulged down his arms, and cut down his flat stomach in a classic six-pack. Dark hair grew around his nipples, and a nasty looking scar ran cattycorner across his abdomen. She traced the line of it with a fingertip and asked, "What happened?"

"Vietcong. Knife was dirty, and it gave me a hell of an infection, which is why the scar looks so rasty. Your turn."

Suddenly she couldn't swallow. "My turn, what?"

"Your top. It's easy." He unzipped her jacket and slid it off her shoulders. Next he gripped the lower edge of her shirt and pulled it up and over her head, tugging to get it off.

Her breasts tensed with wanting him, and her nipples hardened into buds of lust.

"Take your bra off." His voice was gravelly.

Before she could lose her nerve, she yanked the black sports bra over her head.

His gaze on her was hot, full of need. He extended a fingertip to circle first one nipple then the next. With a moan, he surged toward her and filled his hands with her breasts. Kisses fell on her face, lips, and shoulders before he bent and took a nipple into his mouth, sucking like a starving man.

His mouth on her delicate flesh did crazy things to the magical place between her legs, and she moved a hand there, intending to do what she always did, bring herself off.

He dragged her hand away and moved his mouth from her body long enough to speak. "I say when you come tonight."

The thought of him controlling her body that way was scary and thrilling. She reached for the front of his pants, intent on seeing what an aroused man looked like in the flesh. He made a decidedly male sound again when she unbuttoned and unzipped him, shoving his pants and shorts down his legs. He'd apparently left his boots downstairs along with his jacket.

His cock jutted from a mat of black curls. Hot, hard, and enormous, she wrapped both hands around it, amazed by how it felt. He let her hold him for a long moment, before untangling her hands from his body and unfastening her pants, which he slid down her legs, followed by her panties that had turned into a sodden lump of nylon.

She was expecting a heated embrace, so it surprised her when he slapped her rump smartly.

"Into the tub, wench."

Honor had been so intent on Milton's body, she'd all but forgotten about the tub. Her body ached for release. "Maybe, couldn't we—?" she stammered and felt her cheeks heat with embarrassment and need.

"Tub. Now. As you pointed out, neither of us smell all that swift. I want to take my time with you. And I want you hungry for me, begging for me. Hell, woman. You'll be carving my name in every bedpost around before we're through."

The visual that went with his words struck her as funny, and she giggled. Still chortling, she lowered herself into the steaming water. He made his way down the steps into the deep tub and shut off the water. Next he grabbed a washcloth and soap, along with a bottle of shampoo, from a small bamboo table near the tub. Moving behind her, he sank to sit in the hot water.

"God, that feels good." He wrapped his arms around her and took her breasts in his hands again. "You feel good. Too damned good."

She arched into his touch, and her nipples turned to marbles. His cock pressed against her back, and she reached around to cradle him in her hands. He slathered soap over her, rinsed it off with the cloth, all the while touching her nipples or her clit, but he drew back when she got close to an orgasm.

Gasping and panting, she moved her hand up and down his shaft behind her. "Two can play that game." She gritted the words out.

"Duck your head. Your hair's still dirty."

She let go of him long enough to let him wash her hair. It was the first time anyone else ever laid hands on her—that she remembered, and she adored being coddled and taken care of. It made her almost as hot as his hands on her while he nipped the junction where her neck rose from her shoulders.

"What about your hair?" she asked breathlessly.

In answer, he pushed her forward so he could wet his hair. In a few moments, he'd soaped and rinsed it. "Mine's easier because it's short." He slicked it back from his face.

Honor glanced at the water that had taken on a grayish hue. "Ick, we need clean water."

"No, we need to get out." He pulled the plug, and the water made little sucking noises as it started down the drain.

He rose with water sheeting down his stunning body. The slabs of muscle didn't stop with his stomach. His thighs and calves bulged in Greek god lines. Milton slipped his hands under her arms and lifted her first to her feet and then out of the water, so she stood on the edge of the tub. Letting go, he vaulted out after her.

He twitched a towel off a rack and wrapped it around her, soaking up water as he went. Sweeping an arm between them, he picked her up as if she weighed nothing. With her cradled firmly against him, he carried her into the bedroom and laid her across the bed.

"Christ, you're perfect." He stood over her, cock still rigidly at attention as his gaze traveled the length of her body.

She tried to talk, but all that came out was a croak, so she switched to telepathy. *"No. You're the perfect one."*

He sat next to her and traced the lines of breast and belly with his hands before trailing kisses across her abdomen. Her legs fell apart, and he pushed them that much farther as he settled his mouth over her center, just breathing on her swollen tissue. Her hips bucked, trying to get closer to his mouth.

He moved so he knelt between her legs and tucked both hands under her butt, raising her to mouth level. When he licked a single swipe across her clit, she shrieked and writhed, wanting more.

Another lick.

Then one more.

He licked faster, slowing when she was within a heartbeat of coming. Finally, she grabbed his head between her hands and pushed her vulva upward. He surrounded her clit with his mouth and sucked her engorged nub.

The climax brewing for the last hour exploded from her, leaving her breathless, shaken, and desperate for more of him. He moved his mouth from her streaming pussy and traded it for the head of his cock planted firmly at the opening to her body.

"Put your legs on my shoulders."

She lifted her legs, draping them over him and opening herself for his cock. As she watched, he sank slowly inside her. Pain flared when he ruptured her membranes, but it was fleeting. He rubbed her hot center and drove himself the rest of the way inside her, stopping once fully encased.

She wriggled, entranced by the sensation of being full to the gunnels with a cock. Certain movements intensified things, and she repeated them.

"You're smiling." He grinned down at her, hands on her hips as he raised her body to meet his.

"So are you."

"Why wouldn't I be? I have a goddess in my bed."

Flustered by the unexpected compliment, she looked away.

"They're not just words, Honor. Trust them. Trust me."

"I do. The feeling is different. Deeper. Can I come like this?"

"Let's find out." A mischievous catch lit his voice. He pulled most of the way out and swirled his cock in tantalizing circles before impaling her again. In the midst of his long, slow strokes, her body dissolved in a pool of heat, and a shockingly strong climax rippled through her.

"Hold onto the high point," he rasped. "You can turn it into another climax."

She clung to the last of the spasms, and he drove into her faster, harder, until the room spun with light and sensation. Another climax roared out of her, as he swelled even larger, followed by a flood of liquid heat as he released.

Honor watched his body as he came. His muscles were corded into knots, and his head was thrown back. Triumphant whoops rang out, and she smiled when she realized it was both of them shrieking their delight.

Time slowed, and he lowered himself atop her, turning them onto their sides. "Sleep, darling," he murmured. "We'll sort every-thing out in the morning."

"It's probably not all that far away," she said.

"Means you need to sleep fast. We should've used a condom. I'll see we have plenty for next time."

Next time.

She liked the sound of that as she fell asleep nestled in the shelter of his arms.

118

The insistent screech of his phone woke Milton, and he patted the nightstand, hunting for it—except it wasn't there. Alert instantly, a carryover from his years as a field soldier sleeping in hastily dug trenches, he swung his legs over the edge of the bed and followed the sound downstairs to where he'd left his jacket slung over a chair.

"What?" he barked.

"Bad news." Roy's voice held a grim edge.

"Don't stop there, Kincaid." Milton glanced out a window to see the sky just beginning to lighten with the first rays of a gray dawn.

"Grafton and Clarksburg sustained heavy bomb damage."

"They're close to Keyser, huh?"

"Yeah, only about a hundred miles southwest. I called in my team, and Glory's alerted the women and the two freaks we gave a free ride to yesterday. Maybe they know something."

"Be there in ten." Milton disconnected, not bothering to wait for Roy to say goodbye.

Footsteps clattered down the stairs, and a totally nude Honor blinked sleepily at him. "I heard that. Find me some sweats or something."

Milton gave her lithe, lean body a suggestive look, but they didn't have time do to anything except get dressed and hightail it to the conference room. "It's a waste to cover all that perfection, but follow me."

"Maybe this is a good thing," she said as she trailed back up the stairs after him.

"How so?" He tugged socks, a pair of thick, stretchy tights, a long-sleeved T-shirt, and a fleece hoodie out of a drawer and handed the things to her. Everything but the socks had a CIA logo.

She laid them over a chair and shook her head.

"What?" he asked. "Color not right?"

Her face broke into a bemused grin. "Nah, I adore navy, gray, and black. But does everything you own say CIA?"

"Damn near. Better get used to it."

"Yes, sir!" She snapped off a poor approximation of a salute and detoured into the bathroom, where he heard water running. When she returned, her hair was brushed and her face damp. She started getting dressed, something he'd accomplished while she was in the bathroom. "Sheesh." She pulled the clothing on. I'm surprised your underwear doesn't have *CIA Operative* stamped on it."

"You're still harping about that? Do I hear a complaint?"

"No. We need to hurry."

He led the way downstairs and out into a chilly morning where he broke into a fast jog. She paced him, and he said, "You never told me how the freaks turning the US into a battleground is a good thing."

"That part isn't, but the fact that they struck so close to home suggests they're not thinking very smart."

"It's not their home anymore," Milton pointed out. "They'll have to go elsewhere."

"Still, we've made a point of keeping our existence very low key. To have their compound go up in smoke—which surely had to be noticed—and then to stage an attack so close." She paused, clearly organizing her thoughts. "How could anyone see it as anything other than revenge?"

They reached Milton's office building and passed through the scanner on their way to the stairwell. "Could there be any advantage to announcing their presence?" he asked.

"None that I can see." Honor went through the door he held open and trotted down the hall toward the large meeting room past his office. "One of the reasons we tried to maintain invisibility is there are way more of you than us. That hasn't changed."

He walked into the meeting room. Everyone else was already there hovering around the coffee pot set up at the far end of the room. "Coffee?" He twisted to meet Honor's gaze.

"Sure, but I can get my own."

"Do we have damage reports?" Milton asked as he poured a large cup of steaming, black coffee. It was thick, bitter, and strong, just the way he liked it.

"Some," Charlie said.

"They're just filtering in," Charity added. "Tony and I were monitoring the vid feed when the first reports hit. I alerted the rest of the women, except I couldn't find you." She eyed Honor. "Where the fuck were you, anyway?"

"Doesn't matter," Honor mumbled, suddenly focused on adding too much cream and sugar to her coffee. Milton wondered how she'd be able to drink it once she discovered what she'd done.

"What time was that?" Milton strode to the head of the table. "Seats, everyone."

The women lined up on one side of the table, the men on the other. Glory sat next to Honor, and Milton noticed a significant look pass between them. He assumed they were communicating telepathically and wondered if Honor would tell her friend anything about their sexual escapades. He wrenched his mind to their current problem. Honor was an amazing woman, but she couldn't be his primary focus right now.

"Zero five hundred," Tony spoke up. He and Frank were still standing. "Where would you like us to sit?"

"Doesn't matter." Milton glanced at the clock mounted over the screen at the end of the room. "So forty-five minutes ago. Has anyone continued to monitor the reports?"

"Me," Roy said. "As soon as Charity woke Glory, she alerted me."

"And?" Milton prodded. "Look, Kincaid. It's too early to make me pry things out of you."

Roy made a snorting noise. "Patience never was your long suit. The Army and National Guard are on their way to both cities. I'm still considering the implications of the strike pattern—"

"Did they use planes?" Milton interrupted.

"Not possible," Frank said. "We don't have any."

"Then how? Plastique? Did they send runners to plant bombs in key locations with remote detonators?"

"What we think," Frank spoke slowly, "is the first wave was mental. Not so sure about what's happening now, since the explosions haven't slowed much."

"Mental? What does that mean?" Charlie asked.

Honor blew out a tense breath, sounding like an overheated tea kettle. "It means a bunch of Nameless Ones bound their energy together and focused it on something, sending waves of energy to destabilize it."

Charlie's eyes widened. "No shit. They can do that? Destroy something with their minds?"

Tony nodded slowly and pulled out a chair at the far end of the table. "It would take a few men—not more than six—to take down a multi-story building. There were two hundred men and fifty women at our compound."

Milton clenched his jaw, as tension raced along his nerves. This was less than welcome news. He'd take bombs any day. At least you had to buy materials to construct them, which meant a way to track whoever had it in for them. He swept his gaze through the room. "Yesterday Honor told me the men could use telepathy to immobilize and kill. Now I discover they can also use mental ability to take down buildings. Are there any other special tricks I need to know about before we attempt to craft a defensive strategy?"

"Maybe we should take a second look at the data dump from when Glory linked to the computer in her old compound," Charlie suggested, looking harried. He clearly hadn't bothered to run a brush through his overgrown hair, and it stuck out at crazy angles. Stubble dotted his cheeks.

"It's all still here." Glory tapped her head. "Want me to download the part about the men's skills into the computer in this room?"

"Sure," Roy said. "While you're at it, run an in-depth compare and contrast between the men's and women's skillsets. We looked at this before, but I want to drill deeper."

"You got it." Glory headed for the front of the room to merge with the computer.

Milton nodded approvingly. Roy had a quick mind, and he was obviously considering how to leverage their capabilities. He caught Milton's eye. "We need to strike fast and hard. Nip this in the bud before the American public is in an uproar."

"They already are in northern West Virginia," Charlie muttered.

"We were worried about the compounds mobilizing before we tried to free the women from the Keyser facility," Honor said. "I suppose it's possible this attack was planned, but it just doesn't seem like the Nameless Ones."

"It's not." Frank spoke flatly.

"The mobilization data we fed you was a red herring," Tony cut in. "We wanted to fake you out, make you plan for a major attack to keep you busy." He paused a beat. "Maybe I shouldn't have said *we*. Maybe now it's *they* since Frank and I aren't part of them anymore."

"Why would they want to divert us?" Roy asked.

Frank shook his head. "It's that damned V4 batch. They're really aggressive and pushing everybody to side with them. They hinted at some master plan, but the only ones who knew its details were the V4s."

"It's one of the main reasons we wanted out," Tony explained. "The V4s turned into tyrants. Way worse than V3 dreamed of being. They're who killed the women, once they figured out you planned to free them."

"We offered to stay behind on purpose," Frank cut in, "as soon as we knew the others were leaving. Our excuse was keeping an eye on Charity, but we hoped we'd connect with you, and you'd get us out of there."

"I'm guessing my offer of amnesty never circulated," Milton muttered.

"It was squelched almost immediately," Frank said. "If I hadn't been at my terminal at exactly the right moment—literally about fifteen seconds—I'd never have seen it."

"And if he didn't tell me, I'd never have known," Tony chimed in.

"We've been trying to get out of there for the last three weeks." Frank took over. "We used to be free to come and go, but not since V4 started running the show."

"We never were free—to do anything," Faith said, a bitter note in her voice. Crutches were propped next to her.

"Did you stop by the clinic after you got back here?" Milton asked.

She shook her head. "You aligned the bones. I'm doing the rest. Hope scared up the crutches from somewhere."

Glory returned to her seat. "All done. The lists should populate side-by-side on the screen in just a minute."

"Do you have any idea what the V4 group wants?" Roy asked her.

Glory shook her head. "Ask them." She gestured toward Frank and Tony. "No one ever told the women jack squat."

A weighty glance passed between the men. Frank frowned and said, "No, we didn't. Not that this will make up for anything, but we'll tell you what we know, no matter how bad it makes us look."

"That's a good start," Milton growled. "Start talking."

"We'd always planned total retribution for the horrors of the breeding farms—"

"Define *total retribution*." Roy sent a sharp look down the table.

Frank straightened in his chair. "At first, it meant hunt down and kill everyone who had anything to do with the idea to start the farms."

"Over time, it morphed into a generalized hatred for all things human," Tony said.

"Surely you weren't stupid enough to think you could kill off all of them?" Charity raised her eyebrows, looking thunderstruck.

"Not until we developed V4," Tony replied. "At first the line looked promising, but that was before it got away from us."

"We had big plans," Frank broke in. "Up our breeding schedule to enhance our numbers by at least tenfold. Once we had the numbers, we thought it would be simple to strike in key locations—"

"Rural West Virginia is scarcely a *key location*," Roy said.

"Stop interrupting him," Milton snapped.

Roy rolled his eyes and scooted his chair closer to the table. He splayed his hands in front of him, palms down.

"True," Tony said, "which is why we suspect the V4 strain's programming is outstripping their ability to reason."

"They're becoming unstable, like Charity," Frank said.

"Right. Just out me." Charity dropped her gaze to her hands and set her mouth in a tense line.

Milton got to his feet, ignoring Charity's remark. "What I heard is we have thousands of freaks who no longer care about staying in the shadows."

"Not all of us are V4," Frank protested. "In fact, most of us aren't."

"But they're orchestrating things," Roy pointed out.

"Indeed they are." Tony nodded. "No one's willing to stand up to them because they've been killing all the naysayers."

"We need a plan. Let's examine these lists." Milton strode to the big screen with two columns scrolling down it.

～

HONOR TOOK one more look at the game plan mapped out on the white board. They'd spent hours hashing through weaknesses in the Nameless Ones' abilities. One significant problem was computer data on V4 was thin. According to Frank, the latest prototype had scrubbed most references about them. They'd been sly about it. He'd only discovered key data was missing when he'd been hunting for a particular DNA sequence in the compound's computer. And hadn't found it.

She realized her mind was wandering, reached for her sandwich, and slapped empty air with her hand. Apparently she'd finished the ham and cheese croissant without being aware of it.

"We have a direction," Milton said. "Questions?"

"Lots of them," Honor blurted. "The women and I will need to practice the mind meld you're counting on to disable the Nameless Ones long enough for us to get inside another compound."

"Yeah. We don't want them to kill any more of the women." Hope spoke up.

"How long will that take?" Milton met Honor's gaze with his unwavering dark eyes, and she tried not to think about the look in them when he'd been above her, pounding into her body.

"We don't know," Glory answered for her. "And we won't until we start working with that particular technique."

"We'll train with you," Frank said, "since we're familiar with how it works."

"Excellent. We have a plan," Roy said. "Let's get moving."

"Almost." Milton focused on Charlie. "I have a slightly different assignment for you."

"Sir?" Charlie sat straighter; his brown eyes glittered with anticipation.

"I want you to head up the women plus Frank and Tony. Form your own unit."

Charlie frowned. "Sure. Be glad to, but what are you going to do?"

"Your question was presumptuous, but I'll answer it. I'll do what I've done for the last fifteen years: run the CIA."

Honor ducked her head to hide the smile that wanted out. Milton was getting her out from under his direct command. Excellent. A muted noise from a few seats up the table caught her attention, and her head snapped up.

Charity sat stock still, but the look in her eyes reminded Honor of a rat in a cage. She sprang from her chair and raced to Charity's side. "What is it, hon?"

The other woman shook her head and twisted away when Honor tried to gather her into a hug. "Leave me the fuck alone. Go away."

"You don't mean that," Honor kept her voice low, soothing.

"I'm afraid she does." Frank came around the table and stood by Charity's other side. He laid his hand over her carotid artery and angled his head so he could look into her eyes.

Tony pushed Honor out of the way, muttering, "Sorry."

"You get that arm," Frank said, "I've got this one." Between them, the men pulled Charity upright just before her body stiffened and her back bowed. Her eyes rolled upward, and she struggled against the men, cursing and spitting. Saliva flew from her mouth.

"What the hell is wrong with her?" Honor asked.

"Not now," Frank said. "I need to concentrate."

Soon, Charity's body sagged between him and Tony, but not before she'd scratched the living shit out of both men. Frank eyed Milton. "We need a lab environment and AB negative blood if we can get some."

"What'd you do to her?" Glory got to her feet, eyes glued to Charity's boneless form. Faith and Hope flanked her.

"Knocked her out, so she wouldn't seize," Frank said. "The instability caught up with her. The kind of seizure that was coming would've killed her. It's like status epilepticus, but far more intense. Standard medications won't touch it."

"Thank God we caught it in time," Tony muttered. "Good thinking on your part, Frank."

"I've seen this before," the other man said. "Now about that lab?"

"I'll take you," Milton said. "And it just so happens I'm AB negative."

"We want to come," Honor said, joining the other women.

"You'd just be in the way." Tony eyed her and shook his head.

Milton moved to Honor's side. "Take the rest of the women and practice your mental linking. Charlie, go with them so you're on board with their progress."

"Where do you want my team?" Roy asked.

"Stick with Charlie and the women. Maybe there'll be some way to weave your augmented abilities in with theirs. Christ! We need all the help we can get."

"Let's just hope the freaks don't blow anything else up while we're getting up to speed," Roy growled.

"Not much we can do about it if they do," Milton replied. "Now get moving. I'll join you once I've done whatever I can to help Charity."

He made his way to Frank and Tony. "Let me give you a hand. We'll be taking her to the next building over. Do you want a gurney?"

"Nah." Frank hefted Charity until she was draped over his shoulder. "We'll be right behind you. Hurry. It's not easy keeping her under."

CHAPTER 12

Milton stood by feeling like a third wheel as Frank and Tony strapped Charity to a hospital bed with leather restraints. The woman closed on consciousness in waves, her body twitching and shuddering before the men drove her under again.

"I don't need the long version, but help me understand what's happening." Milton glanced from one man to the other.

"Find us a needle and syringe to collect your blood plus injection equipment for her," Tony said. "Then we'll talk."

"You wouldn't happen to have any Cortexiphan here, would you?" Frank asked as he worked on Charity.

"How would you even know about that?" Milton stopped dead and turned to face Frank.

"Doesn't matter. You didn't answer my question." Frank looked up and met Milton's gaze with his unsettling amber eyes.

Milton bristled. He was used to issuing orders, not responding to them. "Most people don't know about that drug," he sputtered, "since it never made it past the experimental trials phase. A few years after we shelved it, it ended up linked to that off-the-wall television series *Fringe,* so no one believes it's real."

Frank blew out an exasperated breath. "Obviously, I know it

exists, and I asked for a specific reason. If you had some here, it would help us fix what's wrong with Charity. You've yet to give me a straight answer."

"No drug here," Milton snapped. "I know where the government keeps it, but the nearest location is New York City."

"Too far away," Tony cut in and jerked his chin at Milton. "We still need that needle, syringe, and injection equipment."

Milton hurried to comply, rifling through drawers and cupboards to come up with what was needed. While he worked, he considered how the freaks could possibly know about Cortexiphan. Charity moaned and thrashed from side to side, and he hastened back to where he'd left them. Falling heavily into a chair, he shoved one of his sleeves up to expose the vein in the crook of his elbow.

Tony readied a syringe, used his hand for a tourniquet, and filled a large drawing tube. He withdrew the needle and slapped a two-by-two-inch gauze square over the hole.

Milton put pressure on it. "Why do you need my blood?" A thought occurred to him. "I had a series of injections to make me more like you."

Frank turned to him. "Crap! We're truly in uncharted territory then. Give us a few minutes to do this. We'll find out quick enough if it'll stabilize her."

"Even if it does, will it last?"

"I don't know." Frank turned away.

"How do you know about Cortexiphan?" Milton asked Tony.

"The scientists at the breeding farms were experimenting with it to improve our genome," Tony replied. "I'd give you a longer answer, but Charity needs Frank and me, or she's not going to make it."

Tony laid his hands on either side of Charity's head, close but not touching. Light arced from his curved fingers. Every time it did, her body trembled. Once she cried out, the sound so pitiful and laced with pain, Milton's heart clenched.

He'd been one of the proponents of the breeding farms.

How could he have been so stupid?

"Ready?" Frank asked. At Tony's sharp nod, he found a vein and injected Charity with the blood he'd pulled out of Milton, taking his time.

More light blazed from Tony's hands.

Charity's eyes snapped open, and she writhed against her bonds. Frank pulled the needle out before she broke it off with her frantic movements.

"Can't you put her back under?" Milton demanded, horrified. "She's in pain."

"If we do that now, we'll kill her," Tony said tersely, never taking his odd, animal-like eyes from Charity.

"We've done everything we can," Frank muttered. "Rearranged her circuitry with our own energy and gave her fresh DNA via your blood to heal her wounded places. This should work."

"Why couldn't you use your own blood?" Milton asked.

"We could have, but yours has more human elements. Even after your injections, it still should have more of what she needs. For example…" He rattled off a string of genetic code sequences that made no sense at all to Milton.

Charity's body strained against the leather straps, and she drummed her heels against the table. "Goddamn you," she shrieked, her face a mass of purple blotches. "Bastards! You're still experimenting on me. Wasn't what they already did enough?"

Frank raised his eyebrows. "Fascinating. At least that might explain why she's decompensating."

"Not to me it doesn't. If you don't have to tend to her, talk." Milton tried to keep an outright command out of his voice, but failed.

"I thought she was just an unstable V3, but from the sound of it, she was one they tried to shift to V4," Frank said.

"Never did work," Tony cut in. "So they gave it up after a while."

"Did you give your people a choice about things like that?" Milton asked, not really wanting to hear the answer.

Tony looked away. "Not really. The women didn't have any rights."

"No fucking shit," Charity shrieked. "At least you're man enough to admit it. Cocksucker!"

Blind fury knotted Milton's belly. He wanted to leave this strange tableau and run until he felt clean.

Honor's one of them.

No she's not. Not really.

Oh yes, she is.

In that moment, he understood he'd viewed her as fully human. She wasn't. Not only not totally human, but the product of a culture that forced hideous treatments on the unwilling. Because he couldn't deal with the implications of what that meant and the uncomfortable mix of emotions pouring through him, he shut that part of himself off. It wasn't hard. He was used to letting his mind lead, not his heart.

Charity's spasms slowed, and she seemed to be unconscious again.

"What happens now?" he asked.

"Either she wakes up, or she doesn't." Frank sounded tired. "We'll know in the next hour or so. If her body's going to shut down, it'll happen pretty fast."

"I'll stay here," Tony offered. "No reason for both of us to sit watch."

"Okay." Frank stripped off his gloves and dropped them into a waste can. He turned to Milton. "If you show me where the women are, I'll do what I can to guide them through the mental parts of controlling us. Maybe then your next mission will work out better."

Milton didn't trust what might come out of his mouth, so he turned and trotted out the door. They were outside before he asked, "Will he let you know as soon as Charity's either better or dead?"

Frank nodded. "Yeah." He clenched his jaw, making the muscles along his neck dance with tension. "I told the others—the geneticists—we were doing too much too fast. Genetic manipulation and adaptation is a process. You can hurry it along, but not to the extent they were trying to."

"It sounds like you feel bad about what happened to Charity." Milton sucked in a breath. "Never mind. Forget I asked. That was much too personal."

Frank stopped walking and made a grab for Milton's arm, swinging the other man to face him. "Of course I feel bad," he hissed. "We were created with human genes. It's part of the problem —and why we can't function like the machines we were designed to be."

Milton yanked his arm out of Frank's grasp. Or tried to. The man was strong, but he let go. Milton's words came slowly. "If you had a choice, would you rather be entirely mechanical?"

"Funny." Frank's face twisted into a grimace. "I've asked myself that more than a time or two. If the answer were yes, I'd still be back at the compound. A machine—even a sentient one—wouldn't be looking to better its lot in life."

"Good point." Something coiled tight inside Milton relaxed fractionally, and he started walking again. He had some thinking to do. Alone thinking, but it would have to wait.

HONOR RACED to meet Milton and Frank before the door to the underground practice area even shut behind them. "How's Charity?" she demanded.

"We don't know yet," Frank said. "Tony will let me know as soon as there's a change."

"Did you do everything you could?" Glory joined them.

"Of course we did." Frank spoke with a simple dignity. "If there's a god who watches over those like us, she's in his hands now."

"Better hope it's a she," Glory muttered. "Charity will stand a better chance."

"I don't want to bat theology around," Milton said. "Have you made any progress?"

Charlie and Roy hustled over. "Maybe," Charlie replied.

"We need your input." Roy jerked his chin at Frank. "Maybe you'll have some way of measuring what we're doing."

"Be glad to." Frank stood straighter.

Honor wondered if there were other Nameless Ones who had a decent core, who hadn't wanted to go along with the program that held women enslaved as second class citizens. In a flash of uncomfortable insight, she understood she'd painted all the Nameless Ones with the same black brush.

"Honor!"

Her head snapped up at the sound of Charlie's voice. "Sorry." She loped to where they'd assembled on the far side of the room.

"We'll take a break in a little bit," he said.

"I'm fine. Don't need one."

For the next several hours, Frank led them through a series of exercises, helping them to hone and focus their psi abilities. She found threads for mind control, and yet others for destroying things—same as the freaks had done to those West Virginia cities. It was different from how she'd used her mind in the past.

Different enough she was furious all over again at just how much the Nameless Ones kept hidden. She and the women had added to their repertoires since leaving their compound, but they could have done a hell of a lot more with someone like Frank guiding them. Someone who actually understood their capabilities —because he'd helped design them. He'd even been able to teach the men some simple strategies to augment latent power from the injections.

Charlie looked up from where he was huddled with Roy and whistled sharply to get their attention. "That's enough for tonight. Grab dinner, hit the sack, and be back here at zero six hundred. We'll monitor the West Virginia situation through the night as well as any other hot spots that develop."

"If tomorrow goes as well as today did," Roy broke in, "we'll move out either tomorrow night or early the next morning."

"To where?" Faith asked.

"Will your legs be healed enough for you to join us?" Charlie answered her question with one of his own.

She pressed her lips together. "We'll see. God knows I don't want to stay here."

"You have to be able to run," Charlie said. "If you can't, you'll put the rest of us at risk."

"I get it." Faith sifted her hands through her hair. "I'll let you know when we're closer to leaving."

"You never answered her about where we're going," Glory pointed out.

"I don't know yet," Charlie replied. "It depends what happens over the next few hours."

Honor strode to Frank. "Do you know how Charity is?"

He drew his brows together. "No. I don't. I'm guessing it's good news, though. If something bad happened, Tony would've alerted me. Just a minute."

Honor felt the jolt of energy that meant he'd reached out to the other man. A slow smile spread over his face, and Honor's tense innards relaxed. "She's going to make it?"

Frank nodded. "Yes. She's just coming around now. Tony's been monitoring her vitals and said she's been getting stronger, and her brainwave pattern normalized. All good signs."

"I want to see her," Honor said. "May I?"

"We want to see her too." Faith and Hope spoke almost in unison.

"Me too," Glory put in.

"All of you might be a bit much right now." Frank looked from one to the other. "How about if Honor visits now, and the rest of you stagger it at fifteen minute intervals. You won't be able to stay long, though. She needs rest more than anything."

"Will she be fit to fight with us?" Charlie asked.

Frank nodded. "She should be. Recovery from these episodes is generally pretty fast. I'll know more once I lay eyes on her."

"I'm ready." Honor tapped his arm. "You know where she is, so let's go." She swept the large room with her gaze, hunting for Milton to see if he wanted to come with her, but he wasn't anywhere to be found.

When had he slipped away?

Was she supposed to go to his house when she was done? He hadn't said anything, hadn't invited her. She couldn't just show up on his doorstep. That would be awkward if he wasn't expecting her. Hell, he might not even be there. Maybe he was in his office, or at a meeting.

Frank eyed her strangely. "If you're ready, let's get moving."

"Sorry." She hurried to catch up to him.

Once they'd moved through the series of scanners and doors and elevators to get them outside, Frank aimed his mind voice just for her. *"It's not a good idea."*

"What isn't?" She answered him out loud.

"Pairing up with a normal human. Particularly not that human."

"How could you...?" Her voice trailed off. "You were in my head."

"I was. I wanted to know why you didn't respond when I told you I was ready to leave."

"Why'd you say that about Milton?" To be on the safe side, she mirrored his use of telepathy.

"He and I had a little chat after we left Tony and Charity." Frank drew his brows into a low, worried line. *"It's pretty clear he sees us—and that includes you, sister—as something subhuman."*

A sick feeling stole through her, turning her stomach into an uncomfortable rock of tension. *"What'd he say?"*

"It was more what he didn't say. And how he asked me if I even had the capacity to feel badly about Charity. Worse, he seemed surprised when I said yes."

Honor heard truth in Frank's words. Maybe that's why Milton

left the practice arena, so he wouldn't have the uncomfortable task of facing her. Of telling her last night had been a mistake.

Her eyes burned with the bite of unshed tears.

"Charity's in this building." Frank tried the scanner. When it didn't work, he disabled it with his mind and pulled the door open.

Honor followed him, feeling numb.

Frank stopped before they got to the stairs and turned to her. "I feel pain streaming off you, so thick it's damn near choking me. Charity needs calm just now. If you can't manage your feelings, present a tranquil front, you need to return to your quarters."

"Got it." Honor took a few deep breaths and scrubbed everything from her mind but the woman upstairs. Charity had nearly died. In the face of that, Honor's problems were petty, meaningless.

"How am I now?" She met Frank's amber eyes with their vertical slit pupils.

He smiled approvingly. "Much better." He leaned close and spoke in her ear. "Never make the mistake of believing they feel the same way about us as they do about themselves."

"But Roy and Glory are a couple," she protested.

"A *new* couple," Frank noted. "Bet you any amount of money, they won't go the distance. Their differences will drive them apart."

Honor squared her shoulders. "I hope you're wrong. I really like both of them."

"I could be, but I ran the odds. Ninety-two point one percent says they won't make it."

She cracked a grim smile. "Well, that's not quite eight percent in their favor. It's better than zero. Let's go."

Charity was propped on pillows atop a gurney that had been rolled into the middle of a lab. Shelves that ran along every wall were lined with chemicals, beakers, test tubes, and assorted scientific equipment. A Bunsen burner flamed under a hood. When Charity saw Honor, she broke into a huge grin and held out her arms.

Honor raced to the bed. She plopped onto it and swept the other woman into a hug. Charity clung to her, and they rocked together for long moments before Honor pulled away. "I'm so glad you're all right." She patted Charity's hand.

"That makes two of us." Charity made a sour face. "What happened to me felt like I was being chopped up from the inside out with hot knives."

"Will it ever come back?" Honor looked from Frank to Tony.

"I sincerely hope not," Tony said. "It was nip and tuck after Frank and Milton left. I had to hit her with a few more electrical jolts, but then something shifted, and I was certain she'd pull through."

"That's what took so long," Frank muttered.

"Yeah," Tony replied.

"Can I go back to my apartment?" Charity eyed the men.

Tony moved to her side and swept a hand from her head down first one arm then the other. "Don't see why not. Everything checks out. We're pretty tough, all in all."

"I'll take her with me," Honor offered. "It'll make it easier for the others to reassure themselves she's fine."

"Keep the visits short," Frank admonished. "She still needs rest, particularly with what's coming down the pike."

Charity leaned on Honor and threw her legs over the side of the bed. "I'm a little shaky," she declared, "but a walk in the night air should do me good."

"Excellent." Honor stood and held out her hands. Charity seized them and drew herself upright.

"Here." Tony pulled his jacket from off the back of a chair and draped it around Charity's shoulders. "It's cold out there."

"Thank you." The look she sent his way was warm, and Honor was glad he'd earned her trust. It reinforced her earlier epiphany that not all the Nameless Ones were arrogant assholes.

Placing an arm around Charity, she stabilized the other woman, and they walked slowly out the door. Once they were outside she said, "You seem more at peace, less edgy."

"It's because I am. I didn't say anything before. Guess I figured I felt so weird because we were in a strange place, but right after we got here, I started feeling like a buzz saw was hacking away at my insides. Turns out it was the leading edge of what exploded a few hours ago."

"Thank fucking Christ the men were here. None of us would've had the faintest idea what it was or what to do."

"Yeah." Charity narrowed her eyes. "I thought the same thing. Guess not all of them are bastards."

"How're you doing?" Honor asked as they set off at a slow walk.

"Okay. We could go a little faster. I'm looking forward to falling on my face in my own bed."

"Glory, Hope, and Faith will want to see you first."

"And I want to see them. Tell me what happened after I checked out. That way the time we spend walking back to our quarters won't be wasted."

"Time's feeling precious," Honor murmured.

"You betcha, sister. You try almost dying. Makes you appreciate a whole bunch of stuff. Now tell me what happened. Did you have any success with that mind meld thing?"

CHAPTER 13

*H*onor made her way to her apartment. She'd made sure Charity was settled with some soup and toast and alerted the other women they could stop in, but not stay long. She walked down the hall in a fog. When she got to her door, she activated the scanner and let herself in. What had felt like a homey space before seemed empty now.

Because the person I want to share it with me isn't here.

And likely never will be, a second, sour voice chimed in from the other side of her brain.

She stopped by the refrigerator and pulled a beer out, popping its top and tossing it into the trash. Brew in hand, she made her way to the easy chair in front of the television and sat heavily.

What had happened to change Milton's mind about her? It must be linked to Charity, but how? She chewed her lower lip, stopping long enough to swallow half the beer. Maybe he was worried she'd decompensate just like Charity had.

The more she thought about it, the surer she was that had to be it. Faced with the ugly reality of what could happen given their trumped up genetics, he'd gotten cold feet. She curled the hand not holding the bottle into a fist and crashed it into the coffee table. The wood splintered, and she drew her hand back. She hadn't hurt herself, but it was stupid to wreck her home because her feelings were raw, abraded.

Honor drained the beer and got to her feet. She showered and crawled into bed, resisting the impulse to check her cell phone for text messages. If he wanted her, he would've called or used telepathy or just shown up and knocked.

"Christ on a crutch." She spoke out loud to steady herself. "I've got to get myself out of this funk. I'll have to face him sooner or later, and I refuse to let him see how badly he rattled me. If Frank is right and Milton thinks of us as machines, he won't expect me to have any feelings at all.

None.

"I can do that." The sound of her words, bitter and filled with venom, surprised her.

Pain made her uncurl her fingers; her nails had dug gouges into her palms. No matter what, she would do it. She'd be the soul of propriety. Last night never happened. She'd wipe it from her circuitry. She was more than capable of doing that, but when she shut her eyes and searched for the engram in her hippocampus, she didn't have the heart to erase it.

It might be the only time she ever made love, and she wanted the memory, needed it intact so she could replay it from time to time. She flopped over onto her belly and pounded her fists into the mattress. She was hopeless. Pathetic. A pitiful excuse for a freak. Even the young ones were better than she at managing their emotions.

Milton rose behind her closed lids. She tried to make his image go away, but it wouldn't, and she drank in the clean, sculpted lines of his classically handsome face, remembering what it felt like beneath her fingertips. Her body came alive with the memory. Before she got deeper into fantasyland, she pulled the plug, forced her circuitry into sleep mode. It was hard, but she let everything go and set her programming to wake her at five.

~

"WAKE UP, GODDAMMIT!" Charity stood over Honor shaking her shoulder.

The intrusion brought Honor roaring back to consciousness. Startled, she bolted to a sit. "Did something else happen?" she demanded, pushing sleep aside.

"No. I'm all right."

"You broke in here," Honor pointed out. "Why?"

"These locks wouldn't keep a determined five year old out—" Charity began.

Honor stood and grabbed the other woman's shoulders. "Why'd you wake me?"

"You'd be up in fifteen minutes anyway. I couldn't sleep, and I wanted to talk."

"Okay." Honor let go of her and started plucking clothing from dressers and her closet, putting things on as she laid hold of them. "Talk."

"I'm worried." Charity perched on the edge of the bed.

"About?"

"I wonder if Tony did something to me. You know, yesterday when I was out cold."

Honor cracked a smile and made her way to the kitchen, where she filled two mugs with water and chucked them in the microwave. "He did do something to you," she called over a shoulder. "He saved your life."

"Beyond that."

"What do you think he did?" Honor stirred coffee crystals into the hot water and brought both mugs back to the living room. She handed one to Charity and set the other one down. It could cool while she sat to get her socks and boots on.

"Bewitched me. I thought about him a lot of last night. That's bad. I don't want to hook myself up with a Nameless One."

Honor took a sip of the steaming coffee. It tasted like crap, but she wanted the caffeine. She considered mentioning that at least Tony wouldn't be likely to dump her—assuming he was interested—but kept her mouth shut. Charity excelled at digging up dirt and would guess what had happened to Honor if she said too much.

"I don't know, hon," she said at last. "Do you think he likes you?"

"I have no idea." Charity shuddered. "And I don't want to find out. I can't go from a lifetime of hating those fuckers to considering inviting one into my bed."

"Oh ho!" Honor furled her brows. "So that's what you meant by *thinking about him.*"

Color suffused Charity's face. "Yeah, it was pretty graphic."

"Want to take a walk? We've got a little time before we're due at zero six hundred."

"Sure. It's better than stewing in my own hormones." Charity rolled her eyes. "Give me a good battle any day. This love crap is for the birds."

Honor turned to one side, so her face wouldn't give anything away and twitched her jacket off a hook. "Couldn't agree with you more."

"But I thought you liked Milton." Charity got to her feet. "What happened?"

"I decided it was a bad idea. Come on." She pushed the door open and gestured Charity through it.

"Probably for the best." Charity trotted out the door. "Remember all that juicy dirt I dug up on him? He's probably got women stashed all over the eastern half of the United States."

"Why not the western part?" Honor quipped, pushing her pain deep.

"Maybe there too. Do you think they'll deploy us again today?"

Gratified beyond words that Charity had moved away from talking about Milton, Honor replied, "I don't know. When you weren't mooning over Tony, did you happen to dial up any news outlets?"

"Actually, I did. No more strikes in West Virginia, but there's suspicious activity in Colorado and Oregon."

Honor broke into a light jog. "Tell me more while we work the kinks out."

Charity paced her and began talking.

~

MILTON JOLTED AWAKE, heart thudding against his ears. His body was covered by a fine sheen of sweat, and his cock still spurted where it lay trapped beneath the weight of his body. He'd been dreaming about Honor. About fucking her senseless and apparently he'd thrust against the mattress until the friction made him come.

He rolled away from the mess, got to his feet, and tossed a towel over the pool of semen, wiping it away. After a wretched night, this didn't make it any better. He'd been worse than a coward to slip away from the practice arena while the others were deeply engrossed in working through glitches in their newly developing abilities.

But he hadn't been ready to face Honor with his emotions churned to shit over Charity's breakdown and the men's cavalier attitude. They'd clearly dealt with the fallout from genetic manipulations that hadn't worked out as planned for years.

He tromped across the length of the second floor to the bathroom and got under the shower. Hot water helped, but he still felt like warmed over mush. What the hell happened to his icy veneer? The one that had carried him through unpredictable situations before?

The answer flattened him while he was toweling off. He'd never opened the secret parts of himself—to anyone. Never let anyone get under his skin enough that their presence or absence meant shit. Not since he'd lied about his age, enlisted in the Marines, and ended up working solo in the jungles of Southeast Asia. He'd blamed Maggie's immaturity for the failure of his third marriage, but the unvarnished truth was he'd been responsible for all his marital failures. He'd never been even marginally emotionally available. Sick to death of trying to batter their way through his impenetrable defenses, the women burned out and eventually left.

What was different about Honor? Why was he so taken with her that she was practically all he could think about? Kissing her in his office had been wildly out of character for him. His invitation to his bed was too. She was the first woman to grace his home since Maggie's abrupt departure. He'd always maintained a strict distance between who he was at work and his sexual dalliances, preferring the privacy of motels and nameless, faceless women he found through discreet services catering to men who needed to remain anonymous. They never knew who he was, and he hadn't cared who they were.

He grimaced. Cutting to the chase, he'd been one bloodless motherfucker. Not much better than the freaks, when you got right down to it. The barricades around his heart had finally come home to roost—and fucked him royally. Opening himself to anyone felt so fraught with risk, he'd bolted like a skittish colt the moment things with Honor looked less than perfect.

Nothing changed with her. Not really. I'm just seeing more of what the freaks are, and it shocked me.

He shook his head. He'd been more than shocked. Horrified and disgusted cut closer to the reality.

Milton realized he'd finished dressing and made his way downstairs. He glanced at the clock. Five a.m. He had time, so he poured himself a cup of coffee. It was yesterday's, but he zapped it in the microwave. He dropped into a chair and slurped the dark brew, hunting for a lift.

Recognition of what a son of a bitch he'd been didn't sit well. Christ! He owed his wives a major apology, but it was years late and better left alone at this point. He could apologize to Honor, though. He wasn't quite certain what to say, but leaving her hanging after what they'd shared the night before last was something he at least had a good chance of rectifying.

While he finished the coffee, he thought more about Frank and Tony as they worked over Charity, trying to save her life. He and the others who'd been proponents of the breeding farms in the first place, had handed the genetically altered humans an incredibly raw deal. How could he possibly blame them for playing the ball where it lay? Even natural selection, when it manifested in the real world, created anomalies. But the timeframe was so much longer, they weren't that noticeable.

A group of eager scientists turned loose in a previously verboten playpen—the human genome with live test subjects—provided fertile ground for the disaster that had ensued. Their early errors were stark testament to the pitfalls, but everyone had been so stoked by the successes, failures were swept under the proverbial rug.

"And here we are," he muttered, dropping his cup on the table with a *clank* and getting to his feet. "They've done the best they could with the hand we dealt them. How the fuck can I judge? I'm worse than they ever dreamed of being, since I never made even the slightest fuss about possibly pulling the plug on the farms."

Another glance at the clock. Five thirty. He probably wouldn't wake Honor if he sent her a text. Maybe they could catch a few minutes before the zero six hundred meeting. Feeling hopeful, he grabbed his phone and tapped out *Can we meet outside the practice building in ten minutes?* He looked it over for a second and hit send.

He gathered up a hat and gloves and went back to his phone, but the screen was empty. Did she not get the message? Maybe she was in the shower, or out for a run.

Or maybe she's furious and decided I'm not worth the effort.

He clenched his jaw into a determined line. It was the conclusion his wives came to, so why not Honor? She was scary smart. It wouldn't take her years to decide to ditch him.

He stomped out his front door, yanking it shut so hard it clanked against its frame. Pissed at himself, determined to make amends, he broke into a fast jog, heading for the building that housed the practice arena. She had to hear him out. Maybe he'd blown his only chance with her, but he couldn't get his mind around it. *Crap!* It had only been one night. He might've been called into a meeting...

I'm making excuses for my behavior.

Not a good idea.

As he closed on the building, two figures ran from the other direction in the predawn gloom. Honor and Charity. He was in luck. "Morning, ladies!" He forced a cheerful note into his greeting.

"Morning," they called back.

"Honor. Could I see you for a minute?"

The women drew abreast of him. Honor's green eyes skittered away. "I report to Charlie now. If you need anything from me, let him know."

"Honor, please—"

But she raced after Charity and on into the building, leaving him with his breath pluming in the cold air. At least that settled one thing. Not only was she furious with him. She'd cut him out of her life.

Just like that. Without even giving him a chance to explain.

Anger bubbled, and the acid from the coffee etched into his stomach. Part of him welcomed the fury. He could channel it into action. Another part of him mourned. If he couldn't get past his own defenses, how the fuck could he ever beg her to forgive him? Obviously she'd sensed his ambivalence. Or maybe she'd gotten an earful from Frank. He and Tony were very sharp. They'd thrown their lot in with normal humans because they were desperate, not because they wanted to *be* fully human.

Once kindled, fury blazed hot, overcoming his attempt at rationality. How dare she? It wasn't as if he'd been out fucking someone else last night. He fisted a hand and slammed it into the building wall. Scraped and bloody, he did it again. Physical pain was welcome, much easier than what was eating him up inside.

He had to either get a better grip on himself or skip the zero six hundred meeting.

He forced his fist next to his body before he could smash it into the wall again. Not showing up wasn't a viable option. He had to be there since the two teams were going to map out their next moves. Milton sucked cold air. He let it bathe his lungs and imagined himself inhaling emotional neutrality.

That's it, he urged silently. *Breathe in strength, breath out tension. This is a piece of cake.*

Is it really? A different voice inside him challenged.

"No," he muttered under his breath, "but I can't let that matter."

He cloaked himself in carefully constructed detachment and made his way into the building. Roy and Glory caught up to him when he was waiting for the elevator. They seemed so happy, he found himself looking away.

"You all right this morning, boss?" Roy directed his discerning gaze Milton's way.

"Why wouldn't I be?" Milton growled.

"At least he sounds like himself." Glory rolled her eyes. "Here's the elevator. Let's do this."

CHAPTER 14

*H*onor walked slowly back to the building where she lived. The others were going to dinner together, but she'd bowed out. The stress of keeping up a staunch front all day had been grueling, and she needed some time to herself where she could sink into a funk.

Milton hadn't disappeared today.

Of course not.

He'd been front and center all day, but when he'd looked at her, his eyes had been flat, devoid of warmth. Nothing like when he'd asked her to talk with him early in the morning. His gaze held pleading then.

I shot him down, and now he truly is done with me.

She wondered what he wanted to talk about that morning. Probably just a courtesy notice that they'd made a mistake. Maybe he needed a night to himself to figure that out. When she'd sidestepped him, he figured she was good with it and dropped any pretense she ever meant anything to him.

She let herself into her home and gathered what Charlie told them to bring. They were supposed to eat, grab a nap, and assemble at twenty-two hundred for a final briefing. They'd fly out after that.

The Nameless Ones' headquarters were deep in the Colorado Rockies, not too far from the town of Leadville.

She and the women had exchanged looks after listening to Frank and Tony map out what they saw as the best approach to disable further plans the Nameless Ones might have. None of the women had the faintest idea any sort of headquarters existed, let alone its location. According to Frank and Tony, if they knocked out the leaders, and made certain the others were aware of the amnesty offer, maybe they could derail what was beginning to look like a series of strikes designed to maximize loss of human life.

Milton, Roy, and Charlie had peppered the men with questions, but in the end they'd agreed to the plan. The Leadville facility was smaller, with only a hundred or so residents and no women. So that was one less worry. They wouldn't have to keep the V4s from killing anyone at the compound.

Unless they had some sort of built in suicide switch.

Honor thought it likely, and she'd even mentioned it. After some level of debate, consensus was they had to move in anyway. It would be a damned shame if all the V4s killed themselves, but it would have the same net effect of lessening the chokehold they had on the rest of the freaks.

"Shit! Now I'm calling us freaks too." She pulled her dinner out of the microwave, peeled the rest of the paper off it, and sat at her small kitchen table. The frozen meal tasted like paste, but she was hunting for calories, not enjoyment. In truth, it felt as if she'd never enjoy anything again.

After eating, she tossed her dish in the trash and her fork in the sink. Thirsty, she bent to drink from the cold water tap. Who the hell was she? She didn't see herself as fully human, but she'd never seen herself as a freak, either. Maybe some in-between species? Certainly nothing like the Nameless Ones. No wonder Charity was spooked by her attraction to Tony.

Honor exhaled long and loud and lay down on the couch. She

instructed her mind to enter sleep mode and wake her after an hour. That should be long enough.

No one stood over her shaking her when she opened her eyes after sixty minutes and glanced out a window at a black sky shot with stars. Moving on autopilot, she layered on warm field gear. That done, she packed a rucksack with what she'd drawn together earlier, and made her way to the helipad. Before their dinner break, Faith insisted she was healed enough to go, but Honor saw the worried look on Charlie's face.

She was halfway across the Langley campus when Faith, Hope, and Charity caught up to her. They weren't moving very fast. "How are you?" Honor eyed Faith.

"We tried to get her to stay behind," Hope said. "No way in hell can she run. She can barely walk faster than a wounded dog."

"At least they have four legs to spread the effort." Pain wove beneath Faith's voice, and she ground to a halt. "You win. I wanted to give my legs a test. They're better. The breaks are healing, but there are still fragile places in the bones. If I stress them, they'll just break all over again."

"Does that mean you're heading back to the bunkhouse?" Charity asked.

Faith made a snorting noise. "You and your penchant for old Westerns. I'll see you off first, and then I'll go back to bed." Her face grew serious. "I want to see each of you again. No heroics. The fucking Nameless Ones aren't worth your lives. Not now or ever."

"Got it." Honor closed for a quick hug.

"By the time you get back, I truly will be well enough to fight," the other woman said. "It beats worrying myself sick about you from here."

"I heard that." Glory joined them. "Couldn't agree more."

"Where's Roy?" Honor asked.

"He needed to square some things with Milton, and then he'll meet us at the helipad."

"Is Milton coming with us?" The words slipped out before Honor could rein them in.

Charity shot a knowing leer her way. "Not quite over him, huh?"

"Leave her alone," Hope said.

"We need to move," Glory cut in. "We're almost late."

Since no one had answered her question, Honor didn't repeat it. Maybe they didn't know. It would be so much easier if he stayed here, orchestrating things from afar. He hadn't been part of the team the night Glory and Roy freed her and the others from their compound. No reason for him to come along now.

He was part of the last operation.

Honor wasn't sure if she wanted him along or not. Part of her craved his company, even if he was done with her. Another part ached whenever he was close. It had been a sweet hell practicing their moves alongside him all day. Sometimes he'd been near her, sometimes not, but the warmth between them had fled. It was as if he'd thrown a switch and become an automaton.

Just like the Nameless Ones.

No. Never like them.

She curtailed her thoughts—they weren't going anywhere but in circles—and followed the others into the building and to the launch area. Charlie went through a checklist with all of them before Tony and Frank showed up. He chided them for being late and did it all over again.

"We have a command hierarchy," he said. "I call the shots. If something happens to me and Roy is close, he'll be your new team leader."

"What if we don't agree with something?" Frank asked.

Charlie sent a wicked grin his way. "File it. No room in the field for opinions."

"But what if I know you're making a mistake?" Frank persisted.

Charlie frowned. "Then I guess you'd better tell me." He hesitated a beat. "I may not see it the same way, though. If I don't, you have to play by my rules."

"Got it." Frank nodded tersely.

"How about the rest of you?" Charlie's gaze rested briefly on each of them. After a series of thumbs up signs, he turned to Faith. "Thank you."

"For what? I won't be helping."

A crooked smile lit his lean face. "Yeah, but at least I won't have to keep an eye on you. Get better."

She fired off a mock salute. "You got it, sir. I'm on my way back to the bunkhouse."

Charity muffled a snort, and Faith hugged her before limping away.

"What was that about?" Charlie asked.

"Inside joke," Charity said. "Can we get this show on the road?"

"Let me find out." Charlie faded into the cavernous shadows of the huge hangar, but he returned quickly saying, "Load 'em up."

Honor kept her gaze on the ground in front of her. She refused to search for Milton. Besides, she didn't need her eyes for that. She'd know his energy anywhere. She made her way inside the chopper and buckled in. It was one of the bigger birds, and all of them fit in it. Roy would be one of the pilots.

She was caught between relief Milton apparently wasn't joining them and bittersweet longing for him. Just looking at him would—

Would what? Her inner voice held a caustic edge. *Make me sad and angry and despairing? It's better he's not here. I have to get over him.*

The rotors spun. She settled back against the hard seat and shut her eyes. They wouldn't be in the bird long. Just long enough to get to an airstrip where they'd pick up a jet aircraft. Its six-hundred-knot cruising speed would get them to their target much faster than the helicopter's mere hundred and seventy-five knots. Helicopters from the Air Force base at Colorado Springs would take them the last leg of the journey.

The chopper door opened and slammed shut. Milton. So he was coming with them after all. Joy surged until she tamped it down, disgusted with herself. So what if he was along for the ride? He was just another boss with an opinion. There were way too many of them. She didn't know Frank or Tony well, but she knew how Nameless Ones operated. They made their decisions, and that was the end of things. The conversational gambit Frank had opened with Charlie had been telling. He may have agreed, but he'd do what he wanted if it came down to it.

Determined to watch her own backside—like she always had—she leaned into the bird's motion as it lurched into the air. Because it soothed her, she linked her brain to the chopper's flight computer, enjoying how it kept the complex piece of machinery skyborne.

Too bad this operation wouldn't spell the end of things. No matter how much Frank and Tony talked things up as a close to final solution, she didn't agree. This battle would last for years. Her kind were cagey. Some of those who jumped at amnesty would simply work at sabotage from the inside.

"How are you doing today?" Frank's voice rumbled over the noise of the blades from the seat next to hers.

"Why don't you just help yourself to my thoughts? It's what you did last night." She sounded churlish, but didn't care. At the end of the day, he was still a Nameless One.

"I thought I'd offer you an opportunity to tell me."

"Why be nice now?"

"I was being nice then," he countered. "You may not have liked my message, but you needed to hear it."

"How come the women never heard about this central command outpost in Colorado?" she demanded, changing the subject to something much less personal.

He furled his brows. "Because you never knew anything you didn't absolutely have to. It was a way to maintain control."

"At least you admit it." The surly note was back in spades, but she didn't modulate it.

"Sure, I admit it." He jerked his chin toward Glory. "Your buddy hacked into the mainframe, so you found out why we kept you on such a tight leash."

Honor smiled, but made certain it held a cold edge. "Yeah, because we can do more than you. Or we could with the right training."

"Exactly. What wasn't in those records—because it got scrubbed—was how powerful we could be working in tandem. Remember all those moves we practiced back at Langley?" When she nodded in response to his question, he went on. "That's barely the tip of the iceberg. With Tony and I blending our abilities with you five women, we'd be damn near invincible."

That raised her curiosity. "Why was the information scrubbed? Sounds like it could be a huge advantage."

"Because we'd have had to trust you with your freedom for it to work."

She narrowed her eyes. "Too big a risk, huh?"

"It wasn't my decision—" he began.

"Can it," she cut him off. "Did you agree with it?"

A thoughtful expression lightened the harsh lines of his face. "Not entirely, but I was outvoted. And I learned the value of keeping my mouth shut. Dissenting opinions weren't exactly welcome."

Honor softened her voice. "Thanks for saving Charity."

"It's the least I could do." He looked away. "I'm as responsible as any for the volatility in V4 since I was one of the major designers."

She wanted to pat his hand and tell him it wasn't his fault, but she couldn't find the empathy for something that supportive. Instead she just pursed her lips and made a noncommittal sound.

Frank stopped talking, and they rode the rest of the way to the rendezvous with the jet in silence.

MILTON FIDDLED WITH THE CONTROLS. Soon they'd begin their descent to the airfield where their jet waited. He saw it squatting on the end of the runway like a bloated vulture.

"You sure nothing's wrong, boss?" Roy asked, keying their headphones to keep the conversation private. "I asked you this morning, and you've seemed distracted all day. Not quite yourself."

"I'll be fine, Kincaid. Keep personal stuff out of this."

Roy slid his aviator glasses down his nose, and his eyes bored into Milton. "Who said anything about *personal stuff*? I merely asked if you were okay."

"Mmph." Milton stared at the heads up display, making minute, unneeded course corrections.

"Did something happen with Honor?" Roy asked point blank.

"No."

"You're lying."

"Now how would you know that, Kincaid?" Milton sucked air through his teeth. He should pull rank and tell his copilot to shut the fuck up.

"Even without my amplified ability to pick up subtle speech variations that signal when someone's not telling the truth, I know you slept with her. She told Glory." At the stunned look that must have bloomed on his face, Roy held up a hand. "No details, man. Just that she'd spent the night at your place."

"So? I put Charlie in charge of the women to get out from under that breech."

"Why'd you bother if you weren't planning to keep on seeing her?"

"Jesus, Kincaid! You're incorrigible." The bird jittered, and Milton loosed his hold on the cyclic. "How would you have any idea what's going on between us?"

"I have eyes. The two of you spent most of today pretending the other one didn't exist. Except when you didn't think she was looking, you watched her. She did the same thing." When Milton didn't respond, Roy forged on. "Look. I've been in enough bad relationships to recognize when something's going south."

"We scarcely had anything as complex as a relationship—" Milton began defensively.

"Semantics." Roy waved a dismissive hand. "I saw the two of you making cow eyes at each other before she went home with you. I'm guessing the sex was dynamite because, well…because of how things are between Glory and me. What happened?"

"It's a long story, and I don't want to go into it. Bottom line is I fucked up, she got mad, then I got mad. And here we are. Besides," he sputtered, "these cozy little midair conversations feel too much like chick-chat. Not my comfort zone."

"Sorry to threaten your masculinity." Roy tapped his aviator glasses down a bit farther. Humor crinkled the corners of his eyes into small suns. "Have you tried saying you're sorry?"

"When did you turn into a regular Dear Abby?"

Roy shrugged. "It's Glory. She's made a new man out of me."

Milton sorted through his jumbled thoughts. It might be good to talk, at least a little bit. "Yeah, I tried apologizing, but she wouldn't talk to me."

"She'll get over it."

Milton eyed him and set the bird on a steeper descending trajectory. "How would you know?"

"Maybe I've read a lot of Dear Abby columns." He shifted in his seat, looking uncomfortable. "I'm just guessing, but I saw the look in those green eyes of hers when she thought you weren't paying attention today. She still wants whatever the two of you shared. And pretty badly."

A thin sliver of hope flared deep in Milton. "Do you really think so?"

"Yeah, I do."

The bird bucked as it hit the ground cushion. Milton guided it into a relatively smooth landing. "Let's get this operation over and done with," he muttered, pulling off his headset, "so I can find out if you're right."

CHAPTER 15

Honor rested on her haunches in the cover of a thick grove of snow-covered pine trees. The other three women and Charlie were arranged in a tight circle, along with Frank and Tony. Roy and his team were a few feet away, presumably finalizing their strategy. Milton rotated between the groups, offering quiet additions from time to time.

Frank and Tony used their energy to mask everyone else's presence from any sentries: freak or electronic. If anyone sensed a disturbance, they'd feel the men's emanations and assume it was one of them outside the compound. Even though air support would have been welcome, Milton was concerned it would alert the freaks to their plans, so the choppers left them off a few miles away, and they'd walked to their current location a hundred yards from the compound.

Unlike the other compounds, this one lacked a perimeter fence, at least a visible one. Frank had assured them several levels of electronics protected the facility. Breeching any of them would set off alarms, so would disabling them. The only route in was a full frontal attack through the main door.

"Assume hostile intent." Charlie spoke low. "Kill on sight. We can sort things out later."

"Tell me again why we couldn't have just bombed this place to smithereens from the air," Charity muttered.

"Because they're set up to respond to aerial attacks," Tony said. "They have ways to track planes—or choppers or drones—that dropped anything from the air, and we'd have sustained heavy losses. In truth, it would've been a suicide mission for the pilots."

"Oh yeah." She stabilized her squatting position with a hand. "I'd forgotten."

"Does anyone have any questions about what we're doing or your role in it?" Charlie's brown gaze rested on each of them in turn. No one said a word. "Okay, people. You can do this. Don't hesitate. If you do, they'll kill you."

"What if some of them want amnesty?" Honor asked.

"This bunch won't," Frank said, his voice harsh. "They're the leaders. They'll chose death over capitulation."

"Got it." Honor unclenched her jaw and pushed to her feet.

The other team joined them and Charlie, Milton, and Roy huddled for a few minutes.

Honor's breath steamed in the chill air. The night was clear with a quarter moon and a million stars. Around her, she sensed wolves, coyotes, mountain lions, and a few hibernating bears. The smaller forest life watched them intently, clearly concerned about the disruption in their status quo.

She felt a jolt as Frank and Tony joined their energy to hers. Doing as they'd practiced, the three remained linked and moved forward silently, walking single file through knee-deep snow. At least it muted their movements, and their kinetics muffled the rest of things. Their job at the front end was to immobilize the compound's inhabitants with a kind of hypnosis long enough for Roy and his group to set charges and blow the place up. At least fire wouldn't spread far with all this snow.

Something jabbed her forehead, and Tony said, *"Full attention or this won't work."*

Shocked he could tell her mind had wandered, albeit briefly, Honor cleared it of everything but directing calm, restful energy outward. If their effort worked as planned, it would be like a sticky spider's web, but one that snared minds rather than bodies.

The men stopped before the evergreen forest gave way to cleared land around the compound. The building looked like a smaller version of where she'd lived for seven years, with a long horizontal wing, flanked by two vertical ones. Snow piled on the flat roof, and the gray walls looked like concrete. Psi emanations from defensive layers wound around the facility rocked her, and she had to fight to remain upright.

"The building knows we're here," Frank sent telepathically.

"Indeed. We'll find out soon enough if the inhabitants are as quiescent as we hope they are," Tony added.

"The building's defenses operate without assistance?" Glory asked.

"Of course," Tony replied. *"They protect—and alert the men to any deviations in the status quo."*

"How much more time will Roy and his team need?" Honor tapped Frank's arm and raised a quizzical brow.

"Not long. Maybe five minutes—unless they ran into problems. No more talk. Roy's best insurance is our undivided attention to our task."

It sounded so much like something a Nameless One would say, Honor bit back a sarcastic rejoinder. She was used to talking back in the face of their commands, but now wasn't the time. Frank and Tony were on their side.

She hoped.

Uncertainty engulfed her, but she erased it from her database brain. Frank and Tony practically had to be on their side. They were in so deep, the other Nameless Ones would kill them if they could get their hands on them.

Time dribbled by. Energy bounced between them. The men funneled it toward the compound and draped it like an ungainly dragon with enormous wings. The shape of the energy was visible to her enhanced senses. Where the fuck were Roy and them? Why hadn't the goddamned place blown up yet? She wanted to reach for the other team with her mind, but didn't dare.

"Behind us!" Glory shrieked, not bothering with telepathy.

Honor spun the same time as the night lit with C4 charges exploding. Waves of detonation energy pounded against her back. She fought for balance and sent death spiraling from her hands. She could kill much more effectively without bothering with the clumsy rifle slung over her shoulder.

Nameless Ones poured from the thick foliage all around them. She killed anything that moved, drawing from a well that burned in her belly. She hated those fuckers. Despised them. Every death helped, but there weren't enough to make up for the last seven years.

"Fall back to the clearing," Tony shouted. "Easier to fight in the open."

"But they can see us better there," Charlie protested.

"Do you want to get knifed from behind a tree?" Tony asked. "Besides, they can't come at us from behind. The compound's on fire."

The air thickened with smoke and bits of grit. C4 had a particular stench about it, sweet and ozone-saturated. Honor killed mindlessly, striking anything that came within range. Maybe it was the linkage with the men, but she'd never felt stronger. Her aim was true, and she never had to strike twice.

Bodies piled around them, and a different reek filled the air. Blood, guts, excrement, puke, and mangled entrails. Out of nowhere, someone jumped her from behind, and she fell to the ground with him atop her. She tried pushing power into his mind, but it was closed to her. Either they were getting smarter, or this one had more ability than the others.

When kinetics didn't work, she butted her head up hard and

back, gratified when she heard the bones in his nose shatter. The scent of blood, thick and coppery, rose from him.

"You fucking bitch," bubbled out around blood and snot, and he squeezed his hands around her neck.

She had to act fast, before her air supply was so compromised she couldn't do anything. Reaching behind her, she grabbed his head between her hands and twisted his neck violently to the side, feeling the spinal column give way, but his hands didn't relax.

Desperate, knowing he could last long enough to kill her even though his death was imminent, she raked her nails down the backs of his hands, grabbed both index fingers and bent them back until they broke. He let go with a grunting, gasping gurgle, and she pushed his weight off her.

She struggled to her feet, but the rush of Nameless Ones was slowing. She sucked air, working on getting her kinetics back online, but by the time she felt ready to fight again, there weren't any more Nameless Ones to kill.

"What next?" she yelled to Charlie.

"We're clear here," he called back, "which means we follow the plan, go to Roy, and support them."

Honor nodded. They still had to sweep the facility and do a data dump from the freaks' master computer, so long as it hadn't self-destructed. At least so far, they were doing well. No casualties on their side and lots of dead freaks.

She loped after Charlie and the rest of her team as they made their way to where they were supposed to meet Roy, Milton, and Roy's team.

Milton ran to them, obviously doing a head count. "Excellent!" He beamed through a layer of soot on his face. "Ready for part two then we can blow this popsicle stand."

"Huh?" Frank stared at him.

"Colloquialism. Never mind. Follow me." Milton set off for the front gates that sat awry on their hinges.

Roy swept Glory into a fast hug, and everyone crowded into

what was left of the compound. "Where's the computer?" he asked Tony.

"Likely underground—just like in all the compounds," he replied.

"Is there a tunnel so we don't have to wait for the wreckage to stop shifting and cool?" Glory asked.

"Probably," Frank answered. "Let's do what we can here, and then we'll hunt for it."

For the next half hour, they worked in pairs and made their way through the smoking ruins. Honor started at a shifting, cracking sound and fell back twenty paces, expecting something to cave in on her, but a Nameless One crept from a shadowed corner, hands held above his head. Like all of them he was tall, rangy, and had coal black, shaggy hair and amber eyes. He was dressed in black from head to toe.

Charity, who'd been partnered with Honor, raised her hands to killing stance and said, "Shit! We missed one."

"Amnesty," he croaked. "I want amnesty."

Charity sent a sidelong glance scuttling toward Honor. "Did you hear something? I didn't."

Honor felt power build in the other woman. "Hold up, Charity."

"Why? He's one of the motherfuckers who laid waste to our souls."

Honor twisted her face into a grimace. It was true. He was, but he was asking for amnesty. Could they just kill him in cold blood? "Charlie!" she shouted, hoping he was close enough to hear. There was too much residual kinetic energy in the air to use telepathy. It'd just bounce back at her.

He and Milton materialized in front of her, and she extended her index finger. "He says he wants amnesty. Charity wanted to kill him. I do too, but it's not my call."

"Since when did you turn into such a Pollyanna?" Charity snarled and pushed past Honor.

"Go with her," Charlie instructed. "Stay in pairs. We're nearly done here, and then we need to hunt down that tunnel."

"Why not ask him?" Honor jabbed the finger she still held in the air at the Nameless One. "That'll tell you quick enough if he's serious."

"Good idea," Milton said. "Now get moving, soldier."

She flanked Charity, and the two continued their sweep of the rubble. When they didn't find anything else interesting, they went back to the place the teams were supposed to meet. Everyone was there, including the new Nameless One. Frank and Tony were grilling him, and he answered their questions, but with such a total lack of inflection, he could have been a robot.

"You're certain that's where it is?" Frank stared hard at the Nameless One.

"Check for yourself." His lips began to draw back into a snarl, but he caught himself and resumed a neutral expression.

"You built all these places the same." Milton stepped in front of the prisoner. "Why?"

"Easier than reinventing the wheel every single time. The way your people do things is stupid. A million plans, a million schematics. Nothing ever matches. Think of all the energy you waste hunting down how to fix things. If you stuck with a single design, it would save enormous sums of money."

"Maybe so." Milton turned to the rest of them. "You heard those coordinates. Go. I'll see that our guest makes it there."

They made their way around the northeast corner of the compound to the coordinates supplied by their captive. The metal door was exactly where he said it would be, and Charlie and Roy blew the lock by combining their kinetics. Honor was impressed. The men had gotten much better at leveraging the power the injections had given them.

"Who's coming to mind meld with the computer?" Milton asked. "We only need two of you."

"I will." Honor stepped forward.

"Then you're with me." Milton disappeared into the hole in the ground, leaving her speechless. She'd figured it would be Roy or Charlie, not Milton.

"I can go if you'd rather not." Charity spoke low in her ear.

What do I want to do? I can't just stand here like a ninny.

The other woman had already started moving toward the tunnel when Honor ran to her and latched a hand around her arm. "I'll go. It's okay."

"You sure, hon?" Charity's green eyes radiated compassion.

"Yeah, I'm sure."

She'd just started down the stairwell that led twenty-five feet into the ground when the world dissolved around her. The earth rippled, and she was tossed to the bottom of the ladder where she hit the ground hard enough to knock the wind from her. Wrenching, tearing sounds buffeted her as boulders crashed into one another, and the wooden infrastructure of the tunnel disintegrated. She clapped her hands over her ears to block out the horrific noise, but loud *cracks* from splintering timber pushed past her pain threshold.

What the fuck?

And then she knew. The Nameless Ones had booby-trapped the tunnel, probably against events just like this one, except the bastard who'd asked for amnesty hadn't bothered to tell them that part.

Charity was right. They should've killed the fucker. Her next thought steamrolled through her.

Milton.

He was somewhere in the tunnel, probably buried beneath tons of rubble. Just like Glory had been under their home compound.

"Noooooo." The scream that burst from her was frantic, feral, filled with pain, but sound wouldn't remain inside her chest. "Noooooo," she screamed again. And again.

Charlie and Roy piled down the ladder. "Are you hurt?"

When she didn't answer because she was still keening like a wounded animal, Charlie slapped her. "Honor. Focus. Are you hurt? Because if you aren't, we have to try to get Milton out of this mess."

"Not hurt," she managed. "Let me help. I have to help."

"Okay, but three of us maxes out how many can be down here," Roy said. "These tunnel cave-ins are a bitch. I rescued Glory from one, and you know how banged up she was."

Honor hoped Milton was only *banged up*. A rational part of her was certain he had to be dead.

Charlie grabbed her shoulders and shook her lightly. "Go up the ladder, get an O2 tank from our equipment stash and three shovels. Come back here and find us. We'll be in the tunnel."

"I can do better than that," she said. "Wait here. I'll drop the shovels down to you."

Grateful to have something—anything—to do, she pulled herself hand over hand up the mangled ladder, shouting when she got close to the top. "Shovels and oxygen. Bring them now."

Once she cleared the tunnel, the women ran to her with what she'd asked for. Honor let the shovels drop one at a time. She couldn't do that with the O2 tank, or it might explode, so she took off her rucksack and strapped the tank to it. Before she ducked back underground, she grabbed the front of Charity's jacket.

"You were right," she spat. "Kill that fucker. He set us up."

"I'm one step ahead of you." She tilted her chin at a defiant angle. "I already did."

"Do you need us?" Frank and Tony closed on them.

"Roy said too many of us will make it even more unstable down there."

"That cuts both ways," Frank said. "We can use kinetics to move things."

"And to keep the roof from falling in farther," Tony broke in.

Honor made a field decision. Even though her team leader had instructed otherwise, she nodded. "Makes sense to me."

"Be careful," Charity told Tony.

He smiled, and his amber eyes lit with warmth. "I will. Thanks for caring."

Charity turned away, clearly unwilling to admit to anything quite so personal.

Honor dropped into the tunnel and picked up her shovel once she got to the bottom. It was dark, and the air was filled with floating dust and grit, so she dialed in her night vision to see. Roy and Charlie had moved out of sight, which likely meant the tunnel had a bend in it, one obscured by all the crap in the air.

Frank and Tony flanked her. "We're ready," Frank said.

"We need to hurry," Tony muttered. "Air down here's bad, and it's not going to get any better."

CHAPTER 16

*H*onor moved as fast as she dared. Frank was in front of her and Tony behind. Within twenty yards, they caught up with Charlie and Roy. The men dug through rubble that creaked and groaned alarmingly each time it rearranged itself.

Honor peered into the gloom but couldn't see far because the tunnel was blocked by so many boulders and sections of roof that had caved in. How far could Milton have gotten? The explosion occurred seconds—surely not more than a minute or two—after he disappeared into the tunnel.

"Let's be smart about this." Tony sent his energy in a broad swath while Frank used his own kinetics to keep the unstable pieces from toppling farther.

"No more tunnels," Honor muttered. "I don't care about their fucking computer."

"You should," Charlie chided her. "We need all the help we can get. There could be data on it that would ensure our victory."

She wanted to scream at him that there was no such thing as *victory* when it came to the Nameless Ones. So long as any of them were left, they'd fight. And then she thought about Frank and Tony.

Maybe there were others who were like them. Who were rational, reasonable…

"Honor!" Roy's voice held a grim edge. "What the fuck? We're moving, and you're just standing there."

"Sorry." She made her way through a slender opening between two huge boulders. What was on the other side was even worse. "How will we ever get through that?" She swept an arm wide.

"We have to locate his life force," Frank said. "Otherwise, this is impossible unless we come back with individual oxygen tanks. I'm feeling lightheaded, and I suspect the rest of you are too. I've instructed my processing unit to be sparing of its O2 consumption, but there are limits I can't dip below and still function."

"Quiet," Tony snapped.

Honor listened intently. She pulled more power than was probably wise, given how unstable their surroundings were, searching for a flicker of Milton's familiar energy.

Nothing.

After the longest five minutes in her life, Tony said, "I can't locate him. How about any of the rest of you?"

When no one responded, Roy coughed and cleared his throat. "He's probably dead, huh? If none of you with your hyper-tuned sensory arrays can find whatever it is you're hunting for."

"I found mice, rats, voles, and a fox den," Tony spoke slowly, "but nothing human."

A shrill keening moan escaped, and Honor clapped her hands over her mouth. She had to hold it together, or she'd tear into the pile of rocks and timbers dead ahead, pulling it apart with her bare hands until she ended up buried under tons of rubble too.

Frank dropped his hands on her shoulders hard enough to hurt and spun her toward the exit. "We need to leave." His voice was rough, but it held command. "You won't find him down here, and the rest of us are in danger."

Charlie moved to her side. "I've got this," he told Frank.

"I can't leave him down here." Honor choked out, surprised she could talk at all.

Wrapping an arm around her, Charlie guided her back through the hole between the boulders. "We all loved him," he said, aiming his voice just for her. "Milton wouldn't want us to throw our lives away hunting for his corpse. He understood the risks in this game. We all do, but we signed up for this life because we hoped we could make a difference."

"Milton did. He made a difference." She was moving on her own now, not fast, but that wasn't possible given the obstacle course between them and the tunnel's entrance. "Aw shit, Charlie." Tears welled, but she forced them back, called on the machine part of her. It responded reluctantly.

"You can cry outside," he said. "You won't be the only one. Milton was one of the last true heroes. I've seen him do shit like this as long as I've worked for the CIA. He's always the first to head into danger, and he genuinely mourns when one of us buys the farm."

"You don't understand…" What could she say? That she'd been angry, blown him off to get back at him. And now she'd never have a chance to make things right. Pain stabbed into her chest, making it even harder to breathe and impossible to talk.

"We'll do everything we can to honor him," Charlie said. "He'll have a hero's burial and a grave at Arlington."

"What good is that?" The tears she'd held back fell now, thick and fast. "None of it will bring him back. What am I supposed to do? Sit by his grave and tell him how sorry I am?"

They finally reached the end of the tunnel, and Charlie curled her hands around the ladder. "Climb, sister. We'll talk more outside."

Glory, Charity, and Hope closed on her the moment she surfaced, pulling her body out of the hole. Their questions died on their lips once they saw her face. Honor sucked hungrily at the clean air and tried desperately to hold it together.

"Aw, hon." Charity wrapped her arms around Honor. "Jesus God, I'm sorry. I know you cared about him."

"I did, but it's so much worse than that." Sobs obliterated her words. Glory hugged her from behind, and Hope patted her arm.

"We need to button this up and get out of here," Roy's voice cut through her grief. "I'm calling the chopper to come get us."

Honor pulled away from the other women. "We can't just leave him here."

Roy's face twisted with anguish. "We don't have a choice. There's no way to retrieve his body without an unacceptable level of risk to the rest of us."

"But I can't leave him. I won't."

Roy strode to within inches of her. "You have to. That's an order."

Honor turned away. Standing still was impossible, so she broke into a run and lost herself in the forest. Voices called after her until Roy told them they'd chase her down after the helicopter landed.

THRILLED to finally have finagled some private time with Honor, Milton took off down the tunnel at a fast jog, expecting her to follow. She wasn't right behind him, though, and he'd covered a significant distance when he felt the first indications of instability. The air developed the indefinable edginess it always had when something was about to blow. A quick energy scan back the way he'd come convinced him Honor wasn't in the tunnel—not yet.

Thank fucking Christ.

He'd navigated enough minefields in Southeast Asia and the Middle East that he knew an explosion was imminent. Retreat would be suicide, so he upped the pace and used his enhanced mind power to blow the lock on a metal door just ahead. He sprinted through and slammed it just as the first of the shockwaves hit. He was confident the thick, steel door would hold, but he was effectively trapped.

He slid his sidearm from its holster and spun, fully expecting to not be alone, but the room was deserted. Clearly it had been manned—and recently from the looks of things. A half-eaten plate of food sat on the desk, and the chair had been pushed aside as if whoever left had been in a hell of a hurry.

Of course they had. The computer had likely warned him the tunnel was about to turn into a hell-hole of rocks and splintered timber. Explosions continued on the far side of the door, shaking the floor and creating a haze of fine dust that drifted down from the reinforced ceiling.

He tried reaching out telepathically, but his mind voice bounced back at him. Next he keyed his communicator. No one answered. Probably the chamber was shielded with something impenetrable to sound waves—like steel.

Milton holstered his gun and surveyed his surroundings with a practiced eye. He was in a circular underground chamber with staunchly reinforced concrete walls. A paper strewn desk sat dead center with a well-creased leather chair behind it. The master computer still hummed merrily along, its banks of colored lights blinking at him. As long as he was here, maybe he could gather some of its bounty.

Though he'd never tested his new capabilities with anything as sophisticated as a data dump, he walked to the machine, located it's phalanx of hard drives and worked to establish a mental link. If that failed, he could always do things the old-fashioned way: pull the hard drives and chuck them in his rucksack.

Yeah, but how the fuck am I going to get out of here?

One thing at a time. No point leaving until I've got what I came for.

He approached the computer, keeping a close eye on it. Perhaps it had some way of sensing he wasn't a freak. Maybe the injections would fake it out. The lights kept blinking in the same pattern, with no alteration in shading or cadence as he walked forward.

So far, so good.

He pushed out tentatively with his mind, seeking a way in. Maybe because he was shielding himself at the same time, nothing happened. He stopped and just looked at the machinery that took up an entire wall. Did he trust opening his mind to this thing? Once it had access, he had no doubt it could figure out quick enough he wasn't a freak.

What would it do then? Would retribution be swift—and lethal?

He unclenched his jaw muscles, gaze roaming over the blade array of the compound's mainframe. A neat row of razor-thin hard drives sat on one side. Jesus, there were a lot of them.

"Discretion's the better part of valor," he mumbled and shucked his pack. It gaped open, and he disconnected and pulled drives as fast as he could, dropping them gently inside. Once he loaded them, he'd worry about escaping.

He worked with a single-minded purpose, having discovered long ago that if he cluttered his mind with too many what-ifs, he didn't do as thorough a job with the task at hand. Even if he couldn't get out, at least he could cripple the freaks' central operating mechanism.

Scratching so faint, it tickled the edges of his hearing had him spinning, gun in hand, as he searched the edges of the room for its source. He stared at a section of wall that didn't quite match up with its fellows. Had it looked like that when he came in? He dropped the hard drive in his other hand into his pack and walked to the place the wall looked odd.

He ran his fingers over a ridge that definitely hadn't been there before. Was there another way out of this underground chamber? He touched, pressed, probed, but nothing shifted. Maybe he wasn't looking in the right place. He scanned the floor, rather than the wall and saw a tile that wasn't the same as the rest of them. Lighter in color and there wasn't any grout around it.

Bending, he pried the piece of ceramic out and found a lever. Milton straightened, thinking. It was possible residual settling from the explosions pushed the hidden door out the quarter inch that alerted him. It was also possible whoever had been eating their dinner in this room was hiding in whatever lay behind the door. Did they have a way to watch him? He didn't think so, since the wall stretched in all directions without any indication of an opening for a hidden camera.

Keeping his gun out, he went back to his pack, hurriedly collected the last of the hard drives and secured his pack to his body. Though he'd been alert for movement from the other side of the room, it remained eerily silent.

He considered swapping his semiautomatic pistol for the AK-47 slung over his shoulder, but decided the pistol would be better in close quarters. Less chance of a bullet ricocheting and killing him by mistake. Adrenaline thrummed through him. He loved the feel of being keyed up, of not knowing where the enemy might be, of being ready to annihilate any son of a bitch unwise enough to step into his path.

He tried pushing the lever with the toe of his boot, but couldn't get the angle right. Settling into a squat, he tugged it toward him, pulling hard. With a scraping, squealing noise, the wall moved inward. Milton sent up a silent prayer that this tunnel was still intact. He hadn't bothered to check outside the main door into the underground room. It led into the compound, and he knew what he'd find up there. Wreckage. The tunnel had to be choked with it, just like the other passageway that had nearly spelled his doom.

He'd dig his way out if he had to, but it wasn't his first choice. Besides it wasn't practical without oxygen. The air in the tunnel he'd come through was bound to be bad from gasses from the explosives. Whatever was left of the walkway that had once led into the compound couldn't be any better.

When the hidden door was wide enough for him to squeeze through, he straightened and called out. "If anyone's in there, come out now."

Silence.

"If you come out, I won't kill you." That was a lie—kind of. Depended what whoever came forth had to say.

More silence.

Kicking himself for not taking full advantage of his augmented abilities from the injections sooner, Milton fanned his senses outward. He found rodents, but nothing larger. Confident he could explore the newly-exposed tunnel, but not so confident he was willing to let go of his gun, he moved into the passageway. As an afterthought, he shielded himself with energy like Glory had taught him.

After fifty paces, he relaxed fractionally. The tunnel turned hard right, but it was moving the correct direction: upward. Milton came to a place where the passageway formed a T. The left-hand fork was level; the right-hand one canted up. Starting to think he had it made, he moved faster. Surely this had to lead outside. He only hoped he'd make it before the chopper left without him. It'd be a shame to have to call it back.

He never felt the Nameless One until something steamrolled into his back and drove him to the ground. Still clutching his gun, Milton batted behind him, trying to hit his assailant in the head.

"Stupid bastards. You'll never win against us," a voice growled.

"Wanna bet?" Milton growled back. Tucking his gun under his chest to keep the freak from getting hold of it, he reached behind him with both hands, waited until the man rocked forward, and dragged him in an arc through the air, using his momentum to unseat him.

Free of the freak's weight, Milton grabbed his gun and fired from where he lay on his belly in the direction he'd tossed the other man. A muted grunt of pain was music to his ears.

Score.

Milton rocked back on his heels into a squat and located his prey. He leveled the gun, holding it with both hands.

Before he could pull the trigger, the freak said, "You'll never find your way out of here without me. We built this to emulate a labyrinth, in case our compound was compromised."

Milton narrowed his eyes. He had the upper hand, so he could afford a spot of conversation. Maybe he'd learn something. The freak grinned down at him, and Milton rose to his feet, gun still trained, safety off. "I'm having a hard time believing you'll lead me out of here, since you'd like to see me dead."

"Sure. I'd like to see all you normal human shits dead, but I'd prefer to remain alive. I'll get you out of here in exchange for my freedom."

"Why is it you can find your way out, and I won't be able to?" Milton listened carefully for the right answer. He didn't have to wait long.

"Because I can sense things like that. It's part of my programming." He grunted derisively and spat on the ground. "All you have is your puny body."

"That's where you'd be wrong." Milton pulled the trigger and sent a bullet right between the freak's eyes. Surprise flickered in them before the man slumped to the ground.

From long habit, Milton checked the body for anything useful, stripping a cell phone and a tablet from the man's pockets. Satisfied, he made his way up the tunnel. After half a dozen choice points— none of which were anything other than self-explanatory for anyone with a shred of field training—he came to another metal door.

He focused his mind to defeat the lock, but he must've been tired because it took three tries before the door popped open, and he walked into the lightening sky of a new day. It was cold, hovering around zero. He got his bearings with the help of his wrist GPS and determined he was a good half mile from their meet-up location.

Despite being tired and thirsty, he filled his lungs with the chill air, delighted to have made it through another one unscathed.

A raven cawed from a snow-covered fir tree. The unexpected noise startled him—and drove home that he wasn't out of danger.

Not yet. He keyed his communicator, not expecting an answer. Both teams should be well and truly gone by now. He hoped to hell Honor hadn't been anywhere near that tunnel when it had blown.

His heart thudded hard against his chest. He hadn't let himself think about her once he'd ascertained she wasn't behind him. Things happened so fast, he'd been in pure survival mode. Besides, once the bombs started blasting, he couldn't have gone back no matter how much he wanted to. With a hand that wasn't too steady, he pulled his sat phone from a pocket and called headquarters. They could reach the chopper and send it back to pick him up.

"Uncle Miltie! Is that really you?" the CIA operator crowed. "Thank God. We've all been in a black funk around here ever since Roy checked in with the news you were missing and presumed dead."

"It's me. Reports of my death are greatly exaggerated. Christine?"

"Sir." Her voice tone became much more professional. "Apologize for the informality, sir."

"Send the chopper back for me. Or if they've already landed, deploy another."

"You got it, sir. Same coordinates."

"Same coordinates. Don't hang up. Not yet. Did we sustain any casualties?" He held his breath, clutching the phone. His other hand balled around the gun so tight, it was a miracle he didn't fire it by mistake.

"No, sir. You were the only one." Emotion crept back into her voice. "Let me tell the others, sir. They'll be so glad you're alive."

"Of course you can tell them." His voice gravelly with relief, Milton disconnected. Honor made it. It didn't matter if she didn't want to talk to him, he'd sit her down and force her to hear him out.

Just as soon as he got back.

With his feet turning to blocks of ice, he broke into a lope, heading for the place the bird would come for him. If he kept moving, he'd be fine. Too risky to build a fire. Maybe some of the freaks were alive and well and out there watching him. He hadn't sensed the one who'd attacked him in the tunnel. Maybe the V4 iteration had some sort of shielding he wasn't familiar with.

His heavy pack shifted against his back. If luck was with them, the purloined hard drives hadn't broken and would hold answers to the V4 mystery. Frank may have helped design them, but without his computer records, he was dead in the water. It was what he'd said, and Milton believed him.

As he ran hard to keep warm, Milton wondered if the V4s hadn't scrubbed a few of Frank's circuits at the same time they obliterated their records from the master computer's memory banks.

CHAPTER 17

Honor slumped in a corner of a reception room at the Air Force base in Colorado Springs. Her heart alternated between numbness and a blinding pain that made the numb phase welcome. The women tried to comfort her, but she sent them away. The effort of crafting responses to their well-meaning words made her feel even worse.

Battered leather furniture lined the walls, and a television blared away, but no one was watching it. Food sat on a back table along with a coffee urn. She'd tried some of the coffee, but hadn't been hungry. In truth, she didn't think she'd ever want to eat again, even though she was certain she would. In the end, her body's needs would trump her tattered soul.

Outside the windows, the black night sky pinked at its edges, and dawn bathed the Rockies in a warm glow. Any other day, she'd have found it beautiful. Today it felt like an affront. The chopper dropped them here over an hour ago, and they were waiting for a plane to return them to the east coast. Actually, the plane was here, but they needed another pilot. Roy couldn't fly the jet by himself, and Charlie wasn't checked out in that particular aircraft.

Frank lowered himself into the seat next to her. "Just heard," he said. "We'll be good to go in about twenty minutes."

Honor grunted something noncommittal.

"I didn't quite catch that." Frank angled his head to one side.

"You didn't catch it because I didn't actually say anything. Are we loading?"

"Soon."

A muted whoop from the far side of the room made her look away. How could anyone possibly be happy about anything right now? It felt disrespectful to Milton. Fury drove her to her feet, and she made her way to where Roy and Charlie hunkered over a sat phone. She opened her mouth to rebuke them, when Charlie caught her eye.

He bounded to his feet. "Uncle Miltie's alive! Damn that old bastard. He's too tough to die."

At first the words didn't register. When they did, a fresh flood of tears came. Charlie put his arms around her, and she sobbed helplessly, hating herself for her weakness, but unable to shut off the flow. When she could talk, she asked, "He's still at the compound?"

"Not for much longer." Charlie couldn't stop smiling.

"A chopper is lifting off now to fetch him." Roy joined them along with the women, who all looked so relieved, it seared Honor to her bones.

"Are you sure the helicopter's left?" Honor squared her shoulders. "I'd like to go too."

"I'll find out." Roy loped across the big room, jabbing the air with his fists.

"We were the second call from HQ," Charlie explained. "They called central command here first to get a bird in the air to pick up Uncle Miltie."

"Why do you call him that?" It was a stupid question, but Honor wanted to know.

Charlie furrowed his brow. "We always have. Maybe because he's like a beneficent uncle."

"You need to elaborate. I don't have all the human associations to understand that phrase."

"He's gruff, but he'd do anything for his men. And he has. It's why we work so hard for him. He's one of us. He may be in charge, but he put in his time as a foot soldier, and he's never asked us to take a risk he wasn't willing to take himself."

Honor wrapped her arms around her body, still not quite believing she'd have a second chance. Even if he didn't want her, she could tell him she was sorry. That she'd behaved badly.

Frank stalked to her side and shot a baleful glance at Charlie and the women. "Can I have her for a minute?"

"Sure, pal." Charlie followed Roy's trajectory to the door on the far side of the room.

Charity glared at Frank, but she motioned Hope and Glory off a few feet.

"Don't do it," Frank said flatly. "It's a mistake."

"Don't do what?"

"Link yourself to a normal human. He'll never understand you."

Honor blew out a breath and walked to the windows. When she breathed on one, it frosted. She turned to Frank, who'd trailed after her, and picked her words carefully. "I know you're trying to protect me, but not all non-augmented humans are bad. All of us aren't malevolent, either. You and Tony are doing the right thing. So are we women." Frank opened his mouth, but she waved him to silence. "I thought about this in the tunnel when we were searching for Milton. When we pigeonhole anyone—assume things just because they fit a certain stereotype—we do them, and us, a huge disservice.

"Milton's a good man. He may not want me as a girlfriend, but I need to patch things up between us. Failing everything else, I still want to be his friend, and nothing you can say will talk me out of that. It was his call to rescue us from the compound. He could've nixed the whole deal and only kept Glory."

Frank looked down. "Maybe you've got a point. After all, he

included me and Tony on this mission, even after he made his feelings about us clear while we worked on Charity."

"Maybe you misunderstood—"

"Not a chance." He spoke over her.

"Well, how about this?" She crossed her arms beneath her breasts. "We're all trying to figure out how we fit as allies. We've hated garden variety humans forever, and they've been scared of us. There are bound to be some rough spots."

He was quiet for a few moments, his forehead creased in thought. Finally, he nodded. "You might be right."

"Honor!" Roy shouted from the doorway. "Hurry. They'll take you with them to pick up Milton."

She hastened to where she'd left her field pack and buckled it into place. Honor stared at her assault rifle not wanting to bother with it, but knowing it was wrong to leave something like that behind. Finally, she grabbed it and bolted out the door. Excitement turned her insides to molten heat. It was only a short flight, less than an hour. She still couldn't believe she was being handed a do-over. "Which way?" she asked Roy.

He pointed at a small, gray chopper, blazoned with the USAF insignia, settling into a huge parking lot fifty yards away. "They'd just gotten airborne. I convinced them to come back for you."

"Thank you." She brushed away tears. "Shit! I can't stop crying."

"You're welcome. And Honor?"

She remembered proper protocol. "Sir?"

"He cares about you. Don't blow it."

"That sounds suspiciously like an order."

"Oh, it most certainly is." He draped an arm around Glory as she moved beside him.

"Best of luck, hon." Glory grinned.

A wide, matching smile creased Honor's face as she sprinted for the bird.

The flight passed in a flash. She was so happy, it was hard to remain strapped in her seat. Dawn progressed, turning the Rockies amazing shades of amber, crimson, and gold, almost as if Mother Nature were rejoicing too.

"Prepare for landing," crackled in her headset.

She wondered why they were telling her. She could fly the bird as well as them, but they'd never believe it. The skids kissed the ground with the rotor still spinning. She wasn't certain if she should get out. Maybe Milton was injured, needed help…

She unstrapped and peered out the windows on both sides of the craft. At first the snowy landscape was empty, but then Milton trotted out of the forest, looking pleased with himself. He ran toward the chopper, bending to avoid the spinning rotor. And then he was in the craft and making his way to her.

"I'm so glad you're alive." It sounded lame, but she felt tongue-tied. Awkward.

"Honor." The corners of his eyes crinkled with what looked like delight, and he settled into the seat across the aisle from her after ridding himself of his rucksack. "Buckle in," he said. "We need to get out of here."

She sank into her seat and moved her headset back into place. "Why? Are there any freaks left?"

The fine lines around his eyes deepened. "I'm not sure. It seemed as if I wasn't alone, but no one bothered me. Maybe they're licking their wounds."

She wanted to reach across the aisle and touch him, but it felt presumptuous. It wasn't as if he'd opened his arms for a hug. She tapped her headset as the chopper's blades bit into the air, and they circled to gain elevation. "Is there a way to have a private conversation?"

He shook his head. "Only the pilot and copilot can do that. Anything you say, they'll hear."

Honor nodded to herself, removed her headset, and switched to telepathy. *"Well, they won't hear this."*

"Won't hear what? I'm curious just what it is you don't want them to

listen in on." He turned to face her with his old, sardonic smile in place.

To look at him, he might've just strolled in from a social event, not a battle. If you didn't notice the blackened places on his clothes and his grime-streaked face. He pulled his thick gloves off and set them to one side. Next came his hat and the headset.

She heaved a huge sigh and dove in. *"When I was convinced you were dead, all I could think about was that I shouldn't have blown you off the morning we left. I was angry because you disappeared the night before, and I wanted to hurt you back."*

He snaked a hand across the narrow aisle and laid it over one of hers. *"Actually, it's me who owes you an apology. I got confused, off track, when Charity had her meltdown. It got me thinking about my role in the breeding farms, and I was furious with myself. Except I didn't see that at the time. All I saw was that you were one of them, and I didn't know where my loyalties lay. I didn't know if I could spend a lifetime looking at you and feeling guilty."*

Hope flared so hot and bright it hurt. She gripped his hand hard enough she had to be hurting him, but he didn't squawk at all. *"I thought you'd changed your mind. That you didn't want me after all. That you didn't know how to tell me what we'd done was a mistake. So you left the practice area that night to avoid having to deal with me."* Tears over-flowed, but she ignored them.

He shook his head. *"Part of that's true. I did leave because I was conflicted and not ready to face you with my insides in such a muddle."* He turned a sheepish look her way. *"We men like to at least appear self-assured. When I'm not feeling up to the image I want to project, I tend to hide."*

"I never want you to feel that way around me." Her mind voice was fierce, protective. *"I'll hold your secrets. To my grave."*

"I'm sorry, Honor, for underestimating you. This is tough to admit, but I wasn't thinking about you. I was so focused on me, I had my head up my ass. I'll make it up to you, if you'll give me a chance. When you shot me

down outside the practice arena, it was like you drove a stake into my heart."

"Why?"

"Because I assumed you'd decided sleeping with me was a mistake, and you didn't want anything further to do with me." He hesitated, his features twisting into a grimace. *"It wouldn't be the first time a woman decided I was too much trouble."*

Sobs obliterated her ability to speak—in any capacity. She clung to his hand, unable to do anything but cry.

"We probably don't need telepathy. The pilots can't hear us over the engine noise." A worried look crossed his face when her emotional storm didn't settle. "Why are you crying, sweetheart?"

She snuffled and fished in one of her many pockets for a bandana. When she found it, she blew her nose and tried for enough composure to answer his question. "This is so much more than I'd hoped for," she managed at last. "I figured the best that would happen is we'd be friends again." She tossed him a watery smile. "Sparring partners in the gym."

"We can have it all, sweetheart." He dragged her hand across the aisle and raised it to his mouth, kissing her knuckles one by one. "Friends, sparring partners, lovers."

"Really?"

He smiled, really smiled. Warmth saturated his dark eyes and bathed her with the intensity she craved. "Really."

One of the pilot's chairs creaked as he got out of it and stalked into the cabin. "Why the hell don't you have your headset on?" he groused at Milton. "I've been trying to raise you for the last five minutes. Er, sir."

"Sorry. The lady and I were having a private conversation. What did you need me for?"

"I've got CIA HQ on the radio. They want to talk with you."

Milton let go of her hand and settled his headset back into place over his close-cropped salt and pepper hair. He gave the pilot a thumbs up.

Not looking much happier, the pilot trudged back the way he'd come.

She watched Milton as he talked with whoever needed him. Her hands itched to trace the lines of his brow and jaw. She needed to feel his body crushed against her and his lips covering hers. Her belly clenched with needing him, startling her with its intensity.

A thought bubbled to the surface, and she giggled.

He finished his call and glanced her way. "What?" He tugged off his headset.

"We had our very first lover's spat, but we made up."

He smiled, erasing years from his face. "You could call it that. What do you know about lovers' spats?"

"Only what I gleaned from movies and the Internet."

"We can learn a lot from each other." He reached for her hand again. "Between us, we have the best of both worlds. Roy tried to tell me that, but I didn't truly see it until now."

"Those two worlds would be better if we could figure out why the V4s are on the warpath." She chewed her lower lip. "Today was close. Too close. I don't ever want to spend hours thinking you're dead again."

"You never asked me where I was or how I got out."

"No, I didn't. The other stuff felt more important."

"Good girl." He patted her hand. "I'm glad to know you've got your priorities straight. I'll tell everyone once the bird drops us at the base, but the short version is I ended up in the room with the computer. I tried to do that data dump trick Glory did, but couldn't manage it, so I did the next best thing."

"What?"

"Swiped the hard drives. They're all right here." He patted the rucksack he'd taken off before sitting down. "Assuming they're not broken. Those blade drives aren't all that robust."

"Maybe there's intel on the V4s." Excitement swept through her, adding to her elation over having Milton, a very much alive Milton, within touching distance.

Milton nodded. "Maybe. We won't know until I turn the drives over to IT. How do you do that melding trick with a mainframe?"

Honor laughed. She couldn't help herself. "You start small. With something like a tablet or laptop and build up to it."

He laughed too, and she'd never heard anything so welcome as the rumbling baritone of his mirth. "Nah," he finally said, "I'm not the start small type."

"I'm finding that out. Feels like we're losing altitude."

He glanced out the window. "We are. I can't wait until we're on the ground. I want to wrap my arms around you and never let go, but I bet the teams will converge on us, and any possibility of privacy will go up in smoke."

"It's okay." She laced her fingers with his. "We have time."

"Thank God for that. I was so worried I'd blown my chance with you." He pulled his headset back into place.

"Yeah me too." She sent a smile brimming with warmth his way.

"Prepare for landing," crackled through his headset so loud she heard it too.

She picked up her headset, but it was a waste at this point, so she dropped it back into her lap.

"It's none of my business, and you don't have to tell me," Honor said, "but why'd the CIA raise you on the radio? What was so important it couldn't have waited until we were on the ground?"

The line of his jaw tensed. "More trouble. I'm not sure how it'll impact us, so for now don't worry about it."

"You crave that part, huh? The tension, the drama?"

He shot a sidelong glance her way, but his eyes were twinkling. "Is it that obvious?"

"Yeah, but I like you that way. Don't ever consider changing."

"Couldn't even if I wanted to. I've been addicted to danger since I hit the jungle in Southeast Asia. It's a high all its own."

When she glanced out the window, everyone was gathered on the tarmac. "Looks like your prediction about a welcoming party was right on." She pointed.

"They're good men," Milton said. "My men—and women. Many of us have been through hell and back together." He paused a beat.

"I'm one of your men now too." She winked broadly

He shook his head. "You sure are, but sweetheart. I want you to be ever so much more than that."

Her heart took flight, filled with hope, and cracked open. The warm feeling spilled over, and she was afraid she might cry again.

After the rush of high fives, handshakes, and "you're too mean to die" faded, Milton extricated himself from the group and motioned Roy and Charlie close. "Have either of you heard from HQ?"

What he really wanted was to gather Honor close and continue their conversation from the helicopter. Covering her kissable lips with his wasn't a bad idea, either. Unfortunately, duty came first. He hoped to hell she'd understand. He glanced her way, and when she met his gaze he smiled just for her. Maybe she'd see the longing in his eyes. He had too many clothes on for her to notice the erection he'd sported the moment he came into the chopper and saw her waiting for him.

Roy nodded. "Yeah, they called. Thought we'd get through letting everyone reach out and fondle you before we pulled the lid off that can of worms."

"Report!" Milton barked, anxious to get the next part over with and find out how long it would be before he could drag Honor off somewhere private. "They called me *en route*," he went on, "but mostly to say you'd have the details. They also said not to plan on coming home anytime soon, but they always overreact."

"Leadville's gone up like it was made of matchsticks. They're considering the wisdom of evacuating Denver right now," Roy said.

"What makes anyone think the freaks will target another city in Colorado?" Milton thought about it as he spoke. "I can see them torching Leadville as pure retaliation, since it was the closest town, but why wouldn't they choose someplace where they could cripple critical military operations? Like Seattle or Portland or San Francisco? San Diego?"

"Can't answer that, boss," Charlie said.

"Did either of you pick Frank or Tony's brains?"

"No," Roy replied. "And we should have."

"Let's do this," Milton suggested. "I stole the hard drives from the compound's computer—"

"We haven't heard what happened to you," Charlie cut in. "How'd you do that? Furthermore, how the hell did you escape?"

"Later. What if there's some sort of master plan on those drives I have in my rucksack? Our brains aren't designed to merge with the drives to check that out, but I know who could." He raised his voice and called, "Frank. Tony."

They loped over and waited expectantly while Milton extricated himself from his pack and started pulling drives out. Tony whistled, obviously recognizing them for what they were. "Holy fuck! You hit the mother lode."

"Let's see if there's still data on them before you get excited," Frank said dourly.

"Can you scan them?" Milton asked. "Find out where the freaks plan to strike next?"

"We can scan them." Tony reached for a handful.

Frank took the others. "Even if we locate a strategy," he warned, "there's nothing that says they couldn't change it."

"How long will you need?" Roy asked.

"Not long. Fifteen minutes for a cursory look-see." Frank headed for a nearby building with Tony right behind him.

Milton pulled out his phone, dialed HQ, and asked to be patched through to the Pentagon. He disconnected after a few minutes.

"Well?" Roy frowned. "That didn't take long."

"Because they know less than nothing. At least I talked them out of raising red flags in Denver. Everybody in Washington is reacting all over the place." He glanced at the building, but neither Frank nor Tony were anywhere in sight. "I bet the freaks would love it if we went to the expense of evacuating major urban areas. That would free them up to pick a different one."

"So even if we discover a blueprint of cities they plan to hit, how the hell can we warn them?" Roy asked. "Because the freaks use their minds and not actual munitions, they can switch venues in a trice. Without having to transport a crapload of explosives."

"It does pose a problem," Milton agreed. "Hey! They're coming back. Let's go meet them and see what they found."

"Potentially good news," Frank said.

"Yeah," Tony chimed in. "Apparently V4 is imploding and everybody's brainpower is focused on fixing the problems in that prototype. If they can't, they'll have to scrap it and start over."

"So you didn't find any kind of plan or a list of cities they want to take out?" Milton asked.

Frank shook his head. "No. We're thinking the West Virginia attacks occurred to distract you from hunting us for a while. Ditto for all the phony mobilization data they fed into your computers. Leadville must've happened because they were pissed about their compound."

"Bottom line is we don't think they're strong enough right now to mount a major offensive," Tony said. "Taking out their command post will have crippled them even further."

"That could change," Frank cautioned, "but it will take a few months—and a whole lot of luck—to reverse their current spate of losses. At least that's our opinion right now. We might come to a different conclusion after we've had time to do more than a superficial job with those drives."

"Could you have missed something?" Milton asked

"Of course," Tony said. "We hurried like you told us to. Plus, did you get all the drives?"

"I thought so," Milton answered. "Why?"

"Because there were some data gaps."

Milton frowned and shucked his pack again. This time, he pulled things out, upending it. Three more drives tumbled out. "Ha! Slippery little devils."

Tony scooped them up. "We'll add these to the pile."

"Want us to have a peek now?" Frank asked.

"Not right this second. Wait here." Milton got back on his sat phone. He turned away and put fifty yards between himself and everyone else. Once a CIA operator answered, he asked her to gather as many of the management team as she could in conference mode. While he waited, he ran scenarios in his head. Experience taught him it was better when he tossed out options than if the conversation turned into a free-for-all.

Half an hour later, after fielding curious glances from Honor—who'd stuck with the women—Charlie, and Roy, he made his way back to them and gestured for everyone to join him. Frank and Tony had spent the time he was on the phone off to one side, deep in conversation.

"Here's the deal," he said. "The brass at Langley is nervous. Understandably. Frank and Tony." He glanced their way. "Consolidate everything important off the data drives I took from the compound. The women will work with you. Take your time. I don't want to miss anything. And I need to hear about those three new drives pronto if something unexpected bubbles to the top."

"Are we going home, boss?" Charlie asked.

"Eventually, but not tonight. We're going to grab some chow, and I'm sure the Air Force has barracks where we can sleep. Assuming we get through the night without further attacks, I have another conference call scheduled with HQ for zero eight hundred. Next steps will be finalized then."

"What's the advantage of us staying in Colorado?" Charity asked.

"We're closer to the West Coast, in case something unforeseen happens there," Milton replied.

"Yeah, but we have a field office in San Francisco, and another in LA," one of Roy's team groused. "Why can't they take care of it?"

"Sacramento and San Diego too. That's not the point." Milton took a breath. "I'm going to pretend I didn't hear that." He glared at the man who'd spoken. "We're at the top of the food chain when it comes to dealing with freaks. Anyone else would have a steep learning curve."

"Sorry, sir," the man mumbled. "Wasn't thinking."

"Let's get moving on those drives." Charity looked from Frank to Tony and made shooing motions with both hands.

"Pushy broad." Tony grinned. "One of the reasons we kept you under lock and key." She dove at him, fists swinging, before they both dissolved in laughter.

Frank tried for an approximation of a smile, but didn't quite manage one.

Glory flashed a thumbs up sign at the other women. "We'll work together. If you ask me, partnership with the men is long overdue."

"No one asked you. Getting laid has made your brain soft," Hope muttered just before Glory slugged her.

HONOR SAT AT A COMPUTER TERMINAL. The Air Force let them use one of their computer labs, and each of them had settled at an individual machine with one or two hard drives. She'd been surprised by how long it took to do a thorough data dump and scan. The files were encrypted and incredibly dense. The plan was for each of them to organize the data on their drives. Once they were finished, Frank and Tony would crunch everything into a meaningful report for Milton.

She chewed on her lower lip as her fingers flashed over the keys.

She'd seen Milton's look before he went off with Roy and Charlie, but she wanted more than one of his smoky, intense stares. She needed him, but maybe that would have to wait until they got back to Langley. They could hardly expect privacy in the barracks. She figured the women would end up in one, the men in another.

Looking up from her terminal, she said, "I'm done. Where's everybody else at?"

A chorus of, "almost there," rose around her.

Honor arched her back and squirmed in the chair. Her butt was sore from all the sitting, and she was tired. No sleep last night, and it was pushing nineteen hundred. She got to her feet, hoping to get some blood circulating back in her legs and walked a circuit around the large, windowless room. Lined with tables, it held fifty terminals with a chair in front of each.

The door opened. Milton poked his head in and asked, "You folks about ready for dinner?"

Honor glanced sidelong at him. Damn, he looked good. He'd obviously found time to clean up, and he'd traded his bulky winter field gear for a close-fitting black hooded jacket emblazoned with the CIA logo, and dark outdoor pants. Her heart did a funny little dance in her chest, and she glanced away before anyone noticed her staring at him.

Frank got to his feet. "Depends. How soon do you need our report?"

"After dinner is fine."

"We can eat while we work," Frank said. "Saves time."

"What do you want to do?" Milton asked.

Frank walked to Tony's side; a flicker of kinetics told Honor they were conversing telepathically. "We'll get our meals and bring them back here," Frank said.

"How about the rest of you?" Milton eyed the women.

"We're done." Glory stood and walked to Honor's side. "Aren't we, hon?"

"Yep. Me too." Charity stretched her arms over her head.

"And me." Hope rotated her upper torso. "I'm ready to get out of this chair. Starting to feel glued to it."

"Tony and I will consolidate your data. Then we'll hunt down dinner before we study it. Where's the cafeteria?" Frank turned to Milton, who gave him directions.

"We have a plan. You gals are coming with me." Milton jabbed a hand toward the door. Amid a bevy of nods, he led the way out of the building and across the darkened campus to another structure with lights blazing from its windows.

"Where are our rooms?" Charity asked.

"Glad you asked." Milton stopped short of the mess hall and pointed to their right. "That building. You've got rooms on the second floor. Your names should be tacked on plates next to the doors."

"Are we free to walk around after dinner?" Hope asked.

"Yes. So long as you don't leave the base. I'd get as much sleep as I could if I were you, though. No matter what happens, tomorrow will be another long day."

They reached the mess hall, and Milton held the door open for them. Honor hesitated by his side. "Are you going to eat with us?"

He let the door close, leaving them on the outside, circled her waist with his arm, and murmured. "If you don't mind missing dinner with the group, I set us up a little something in my quarters."

"Aren't you in the barracks with the rest of the guys?"

"No. The Air Force is nothing if not bound to protocol. They assigned me a small apartment. Once they discovered Roy's wife was here, he and Glory got one too."

"But they're not actually married."

"Who's going to check? And it gives them some private space."

Unfamiliar emotions roiled through her. "You're very kind."

"No I'm not, but Roy would do the same for me. He helped me think through some of the rough places about you—and he told me you cared about me."

Her mouth gaped open. "How could he have known? He wasn't inside my head. I'd have felt the intrusion."

"Because he has eyes, sweetheart. And he's quite perceptive." Milton lowered his voice and guided her across the snowy campus with its concrete walkways. "To have any longevity in this business, you have to notice everything. No detail is too small to risk ignoring. After you've done it for a while, it becomes second nature. Come on. Our quarters aren't far."

Honor fell into step next to him. "What exactly did he notice?" Honor was confused, sure she'd been more circumspect than that. Unless Glory blabbed. "Did Glory say something?"

"Yes, but not all that much. Roy detected us studiously avoiding each other before we left Langley. Except I guess I spent too much time looking at you on the sly."

Heat swept up from her chest. "Yeah, huh? I looked at you too, but only when I didn't think you'd notice."

"I may not have…" Milton grinned at her. "…but Roy did. We've been watching each other's backs for a long time. Anyway, that's how he figured out something was wrong."

He came to a halt in front of a small, neat building near the perimeter fence and fished in his pocket for a key.

"No scanners?"

"Sure, but only in key locations. Guess they're not worried about this apartment building being infiltrated by spies."

She followed him down a central hallway and through a second door labeled 1A. He kicked the door shut behind them before turning to face her and closing his arms around her. He nuzzled her neck, and his lips felt amazing as they traveled lazily upward to her ear.

She angled her face for a kiss. His mouth was hot, firm, demanding, and she opened hers beneath his insistent, probing tongue. Her nipples hardened against his chest, and heat spooled between her legs. Her belly tightened with wanting the man holding her, needing him like the air she breathed.

He ran his hands down her back until they settled around the globes of her ass, and he pulled her hard against his swollen cock. Time ground to a halt as they kissed. She twined her arms around him, delighted by the hard slabs of muscle running down his shoulders and back. Her hips writhed against him, driven by a mind of their own.

He finally pulled his mouth off hers. "I'm not thinking," he said, his voice low and husky with wanting her. "You've been working ever since you got here and for hours before that. You must want a shower. Clean clothes. Food."

Honor locked her gaze onto his, drawn by need flaring in the depths of his dark eyes. She could lose herself in their mystery and die a happy woman. "I should shower," she said finally. "It'd be nicer for you if I was clean. Don't care much about the rest."

"Shower's that way." He jerked his chin to the left. "I put out towels for you. And there's soap and shampoo. Maybe by the time you get out, you'll have changed your mind about supper. Or at least a drink."

"Did you eat?" she asked.

He shook his head. "No. I waited for you."

Honor took his face between her hands and stroked her thumbs over his cheekbones. "That means you must be hungry. I'll clean up. It won't take me long. How about if you put out some food for us, and we'll share a meal."

"I'd like that." His eyes gleamed warmly, and he played his hands lazily up and down her back, settling again on the curves of her butt.

She nibbled his lips and kissed him once more, sinking her tongue inside his mouth this time, as she wrapped him in her arms. It felt so good to hold him. To know he wanted her with the same ferocity that blazed a path from her heart to her belly. She dragged her mouth from his. "I love holding you."

He captured her wrists and pulled her hands around to his mouth where he turned them palm up and kissed them. "We're so new, it's hard to know what to say, but you're a very special woman, Honor."

A warm, fluttery place came to life inside her. "You're pretty special yourself. I need to get into that shower before I forget myself, strip you naked, and drag you down to the living room floor."

"What would you do then?" The banked fires in his dark eyes heated.

She tried to talk, but her throat thickened with wanting him, and her tongue wouldn't cooperate. *I'll show you, later.*

She turned and fled down a short hallway, finding the bathroom easily, shedding clothes as she went. Thank God for telepathy. How the hell did normal humans manage without it?

CHAPTER 19

When she came out of the bathroom, dressed in clean sweats he'd left for her, with her long hair wrapped in a towel, her body glowed, but it was nothing compared with the happiness infusing her core. Smiling like a fool, she found her way to the small kitchen where Milton had a single candle lit in the center of a small table. Sandwiches and salads were arranged on plates, and an open bottle of wine sat alongside two glasses.

"It's not as fancy as what you'd have gotten in the mess hall—" he began.

She placed her palm over his mouth. "It's better than anything I would've gotten there because you made it for me."

"Nah. I can't claim credit for making it. All I did was select things from the buffet line." He unwound the towel from around her head and draped it over a hook. "Are you warm enough?'

She nodded. Having anyone take care of her was such a novelty —and so welcome—she searched for words to thank him.

After she'd blundered through a few, he pulled her close and strung kisses across her cheeks. "You don't owe me a thing, sweetheart. I love doing things to make your life easier. Now sit and eat a bite, so I can take you to bed."

Honor tilted her head and looked at him. "I thought we'd fall into bed right away."

"If we were normal people, we would've, but we're soldiers. That means you need to feed your body—in case something happens, and we have to mobilize." He brushed his thumb over her lower lip. I'd like nothing better than to shut the world out, take you to bed, and not resurface for days, but we can't do that."

"It's okay. I understand." She smiled. "Let's get to that food. I can eat pretty fast."

He grinned back and moved around her to pour wine into the glasses. He held out her chair and guided her into it.

"I could get used to service," she murmured.

"I'll spoil you every chance I get." He sat, picked up his wine glass, and clinked it against hers. "To us."

"I'll most definitely drink to that."

They made small talk over the meal, and the wine bottle emptied. A buzzy sensation engulfed her, warm and tingly. "I like wine better than whiskey," she declared. "It's more subtle."

"I'll remember that. Do you want anything else? Another sandwich? More salad?"

She shook her head, got to her feet, and walked to where he sat. Straddling him, she sat across his lap, facing him, and ran her fingers through his close-cropped hair, enjoying the feel of his skin beneath her fingertips. "We've lucked out so far," she said. "No one's bothered you."

"You never know." He quirked a brow. "Someone might come looking for you."

"Less likely. Ninety-four point two percent against less than twenty."

"If the odds of someone needing me are that high, we'd better hurry." He wrapped his arms around her. "Tell me what you'd have done to me, how you'd have stripped me naked, when we first got here."

"Mmm." She leaned in so her nipples brushed against his chest and reached between them to settle her hands over his hard-on. "I'd have unzipped your jacket, laid it aside, and yanked your shirt over your head. Once your torso was naked, I'd have licked your nipples and worshipped those incredible muscles you have running through your chest, arms, and shoulders."

His cock jumped against her curved fingers, and he pressed into her. "What then?" he asked, with a sexy catch in his voice.

"I'd have pushed you down onto the floor, unfastened your pants, and jockeyed them down your hips. Then I'd have laid my hands over your cock, so you could feel their heat, and gotten your underwear out of the way." She busied her fingers with the button and zipper on his pants as she spoke. His erection sprang into her waiting hands.

"And then?"

She captured his gaze, still working his cock between her curved palms. "No underwear?"

"Didn't figure I'd need any. What would you do to me next, sweetheart?"

Desire thickened her throat. "Can we go to bed, and I'll show you?"

"Not until you tell me. I love it when you talk dirty to me."

She twirled her fingers around the head of his cock, spreading the liquid oozing from its tip. "I'd lick you and suck you and pump my hand on your shaft at the same time." Heat rose to her face from more than lust. "I've never done that before, but I figured I could mind meld with you and figure out what you like."

"Would you make me come that way?" His breath quickened, and his voice was gravelly with need.

"Would you like me to?"

"It's a tough call. I want to do everything with you. Fuck you, have you go down on me, go down on you."

He thrust into her hands, his cock growing longer and harder as they teased each other. He moved a hand between her legs, finding her sensitive nub through her sweat pants. She moaned and writhed against his hand, a climax very close.

"Please. Can we go to bed and do all those things I was talking about?"

"Soon." He breathed warm air on her neck, nuzzling her, as he ran his tongue across the hollow in her throat. "Do I come when I'm in your mouth?"

Honor closed her eyes, lost in the visual. "No. I stop what I'm doing before you come. I turn around, get on all fours, and you enter me from behind. You're so hot, you push all the way in fast and hard. Then you reach around between my legs and rub my clit."

"Like this?" His hand moved faster, and the climax pooled in her belly exploded.

She moaned and thrust against him, lost in sensation, never wanting it to end.

He moved his hands beneath her butt and rose from the chair with her still clinging to him. She wrapped her arms and legs around him, and he carried her to the bedroom where he laid her tenderly on the bed.

While she watched, he stripped off his clothes, baring his Greek god body. His nipples were hard, little buds of lust, and his cock stood out from its mat of black curls, hard, long, thick, and all for her. "Damn, you're perfect," she said. "I could look at you naked forever."

"That makes me glad." He knelt next to her on the bed and tugged her sweat pants down her hips. Next he pushed her top up, exposing her breasts, and bent to take her nipples into his mouth one at a time, sucking, biting, rolling them with his tongue. She arched into his touch and threaded her fingers in his hair. Excitement coursed through her, and another peak built.

He lifted his mouth from her breasts. "I loved the visual of taking you from behind. Turn over."

She flipped onto her belly and rose to her hands and knees, waiting for the thrust of him to fill her, but it didn't happen. She twisted and saw him kneeling behind her, gazing at her with that heat in his eyes that turned her stomach to liquid lust and her legs to jelly. As she watched, he tore open a foil packet and rolled a condom onto himself, tossing the wrapper aside.

"You have the finest pussy," he said, his voice a deep growl. "I was admiring the view."

She wriggled her butt. "I was hoping you'd do more than admire it."

"Really? Tell me what you want, Honor. I need all the hot, gritty details."

"How about this?" She slammed into his mind because it was easier, and she wanted to feel what he felt. *"Fuck me. Do it now. Do it hard."*

He joined his mind to hers. *"Whatever the lady wants."* He gripped her hips with both hands. She straightened and grasped the headboard, feeling him seat his cock at the entrance to her body. Stabilizing her hips, he pressed inside.

The heat of her surrounding him coursed through her mind at the same time his hard length entered her. The dual feedback loop stoked her lust, and she moved her butt in tiny circles to see what it did to him.

"Christ, you make me hot." He pulled out and slid back inside, burying himself.

"Not nearly as hot as you're going to be." She used her mind to string imaginary fingers down his back. He shuddered under her touch as she moved between his butt cheeks and on into his anus. A muffled grunt from him told her all she needed to know, and she probed his sensitive tissue.

He moved faster, any pretense of control gone, and she met him stroke for stroke. He dipped his hands between her legs. She felt how her slick tissue slid between his fingers.

A climax rocked her. His cock swelled bigger inside her, and she knew he was close. Felt it in his mind and in how he rubbed her clit.

His anus contracted around her virtual fingers, and another set of contractions spooled.

She joined him in release as their bodies swayed together, her fingers clutching the headboard so hard her knuckles were white. It took a long time for the spasms of their mutual heat to subside. He pulled out and got off the bed.

She flopped onto her back and watched him unroll the sheath from his cock. "I control things like when I get pregnant, so you don't really need that."

He returned to the bed. Lying next to her, he pulled her into his arms. "Good to know. I felt bad because we didn't use one that first time. Aside from pregnancy, I don't have anything communicable. The CIA docs check us regularly—for everything." He stroked her face and moved strands of hair out of the way. "That was amazing. Incredible." He pushed his still erect cock against her belly. "I could fuck you all night, but we need to get some sleep."

She smiled. "Soldiers, huh?"

"Yeah, soldiers."

Honor snuggled closer into his embrace. "I'm happy."

"So am I, sweetheart. We need to see where this leads us, but I'm optimistic."

"Hey!" She leaned back so she could look at him. "I'm a romance, not a military gambit."

"Sorry, darling. I know that. But I'm a military guy. You need to cut me some slack."

"I'll cut you all the slack you want…" She narrowed her eyes. "…so long as you don't do something like you did the night you ran off because you didn't want to face me."

He stroked her face again with calloused fingertips. "You have my word on that. We're a team of two, and we'll figure things out together."

"I like the way that sounds." She laid a hand over his and gripped it. When he squeezed back, she moved his fingers to her mouth and kissed them.

"Me too. You didn't ask, but this is really different from my marriages. I never let any of my wives far enough in to mean anything to me."

"Does that mean I've gotten under your skin?"

"It means a whole helluva lot more than that, sweetheart." He kissed her forehead. "Sleep now. It'll be a short night as it is."

Almost as if it were a hypnotic suggestion, but more likely because she was exhausted, the drop into slumber was almost immediate once she shut her eyes.

CHAPTER 20

Milton let himself out the door at zero seven hundred. He planned to nab Roy and Charlie for the eight a.m. conference call. He'd left Honor deeply asleep and wanted her to get more rest. Despite his good intentions, they woke twice during the night, making long, slow, lazy love each time. In all, they couldn't have snatched more than a handful of hours of sleep.

Roy emerged from a neighboring building, twin to Milton's, at least from outside appearances. He sprinted to Milton's side. "Feel like a run?"

"Sure." Milton broke into an easy jog.

Roy paced him and observed, "You're looking chipper this morning."

Milton turned to him. "Mining for details won't buy you a thing, but yeah, we're back on track."

"I'm certain Honor's relieved. You should've seen her moping around the room the Air Force stuck us in after we got back."

Milton picked up the pace. "She thought I was dead. Of course she would've been upset. She had things she wanted to say, or unsay as it were, and death's pretty permanent. Hard to have a conversation with a corpse."

"Hell, buddy." Roy slugged him in the arm. "I thought you were dead. Don't do that to me again. Okay?"

"I'll try not to. None of my communication methods worked from that underground room where the freaks kept their computer. I'm fairly certain the walls and ceiling were shielded with metal."

"Maybe we could implant a tracking device."

Milton rolled his eyes. "It wouldn't have worked, either."

"Kidding aside. I'm glad you and Honor worked things out. Glory was worried. The women are really important to her, and she wants all of them to be as happy as she is."

"Speaking of which, when's the wedding?" Milton turned onto a track someone had thoughtfully shoveled the snow from.

"As soon as we can clear a week. Thought I'd take her to my place in the Florida Keys for a honeymoon and get us out of the cold."

"Will you be inviting the rest of us?"

"To Florida?"

"Either that, or you could have the wedding here and then go south."

"I'll see what Glory wants to do."

Charlie ran up from behind. "Morning!" He glanced from one of them to the other. "Good to see at least some of us got laid last night."

Milton snorted. "You're just jealous, McClaren."

"Damn straight, I am. What's up with the meeting in…" He glanced at his wrist. "…thirty minutes?"

"I want both of you to join me," Milton said. "I have no idea what Langley will have cooked up overnight. Did either of you check in with Frank or Tony?"

"Yeah, me," Roy said. "I stopped by the computer lab before I went to bed."

"Anything new?"

"More of the same," Roy replied. "Thank God. Once I realized there were more drives, I worried about what was on them. Turns out the freaks mapped out a bunch of strategies, but they were pretty vague. More of a broad brush, than specifics."

"What kind of strategies?" Milton pressed.

"They want to rule the world. What else is new?"

Milton turned it over as they ran. "They think like computers, so it's not likely they'd hatch up plans with zero probability of success. Which means they know something we don't."

"Something that wasn't on those drives," Charlie cut in.

"Exactly," Milton concurred.

"According to Frank and Tony, we won't be out of the woods until all of them are dead," Roy said.

Milton ground to a halt. "They really said that? About their own people?" When Roy nodded, Milton shook his head. "Don't they think there might be others like them who want amnesty?"

"Sure," Roy replied. "But the task of sorting them from the rest would require some way of us driving communication past each compound's filters."

"Did they offer up any suggestions how to do that?" Charlie asked.

"No," Roy said, "but then I didn't ask that exact question, either. They're fairly literal, and not big on volunteering information."

"Let's find out before we get Langley on the phone." Milton started running again, this time heading for the computer lab. He suspected Frank and Tony had worked through the night, and he wasn't wrong.

Both men looked up when he, Roy, and Charlie steamed through the door. Milton outlined what he needed.

Frank's brow creased. Maybe he was considering the problem, or maybe he was annoyed by the additional request.

Before he could answer, Tony said, "Yeah, we can do that. Data flows through a router and is transmitted to the compounds. If we set up something to interrupt the filters at the central location—and duped the watchdog in charge of disseminating information—we could push damn near anything through."

"Is the watchdog electronic?" Roy asked.

Frank nodded. "It alerts one of us if we need to alter something."

"Do it," Milton growled. "I wanted that amnesty offer on the table weeks ago. We'll check back later. Plan on a meeting around zero nine thirty."

"You got it." Tony snapped off such a sorry excuse for a salute that Milton laughed.

"This ain't the Army, son. No need for anything fancy."

He led Roy and Charlie into another building where the Air Force Liaison told him private conference rooms were located and grabbed one. It was pushing eight when he took out his sat phone. After setting it on speaker, he dialed in.

NINETY MINUTES LATER, Milton disconnected and glanced at his sat phone's battery indicator. He needed to find a place to plug it in. "That took a hell of a lot longer than I thought it would," he muttered.

"No shit." Roy rolled his eyes. "Christ! Are they always that longwinded?"

"Sometimes they're worse."

"Thanks for shielding us from the worst of Langley's politics." Charlie sent a glance Milton's way. "Like Roy, I had no idea they chewed every single point to death."

Milton got to his feet. "The good news is we get to go home. Assemble everyone in the computer lab, and I can go over our next steps."

"I'll get my team," Roy said.

"And I'll rustle up the women." Charlie winked broadly. "It's a tough job, but someone's gotta do it."

When they emerged into the pallid sun of a winter day, Milton inhaled deeply. He'd always loved high altitude air; it reminded him of his ranch in Montana's mountains. An idea formed. He tugged his failing sat phone out and told Charlie, "I'll meet you there in just a few." After the other man left, Milton dialed a number.

He ran hard to get to the computer lab. He didn't want to make his people wait, and it had taken so long on the phone this time that it had truly died. He made his way to the front of the room and motioned Roy and Charlie to his side. "Did you tell them anything?"

"No, boss. We thought you'd want to do that."

"Thanks." He nodded sharply and scanned the group.

Everyone was there. Honor glanced up shyly, her face coloring a lovely rose before she looked down.

"We're heading back to Langley as soon as we get the jet airborne. Once we're there, report to your duty stations, and work your normally assigned shift." He glanced at Frank and Tony. "Did you get that amnesty offer to go through?"

"We sure did," Frank said. "Wasn't even all that hard."

"Excellent." Milton clasped his hands behind his back. "Assuming they don't fire on us again, we're going to give the amnesty offer two weeks and see what shakes loose. During that time, we're going to train two additional teams in the fine points of freakdom. Langley decided we're spread too thin, and we need to share our knowledge with a few more agents."

"How do you feel about that?" Charity asked.

"It's a good call." Milton looked down his nose at her. "But even if I disagreed, it's an order from those I report to at the Pentagon. They don't pay me to have opinions. They pay me to be a good soldier, and don't you ever forget that, since it applies to all of you too."

"What happens if there are more hot spots?" Charlie asked.

"We'll address them as they occur. You'll continue to head up the women, Frank, and Tony as a team. If we get some takers who want amnesty, we'll form additional teams, which is one reason why training more agents makes a great deal of sense."

"We'll spend more time with those drives," Tony said. "I'd feel better about them if I had a solid week to make certain we didn't miss any encrypted data."

Milton nodded his approval. When no one said anything else, he asked, "Questions?" He waited, but the silence held. "All right. You're free to go. Flight line in half an hour."

Everyone rose and headed for the door. Milton caught Honor's eye and motioned her over. He waited until they were alone. "I managed to finagle forty-eight hours' leave. How would you like to come to my ranch in Montana?"

Her lovely green eyes widened in surprise, and a pleased smile spread over her face. She clasped her hands around one of his. "I'd love to. Did you get the time off for me too?"

"Of course. I didn't want to go there by myself."

"When do we leave?"

"Immediately. I'll have the jet drop us off. It's not too far out of their way, and then we can rent a plane to fly back to Virginia."

An uncomfortable expression washed over her face, and her grip tightened on his hand. "What will the others think?"

He tilted her chin, so she had to look at him. "I don't give a rat's ass what they think, but if they think anything, I hope it's that we're falling in love and deserve a couple of days together."

He pried his hand out from between hers and opened his arms. She dove into them and huddled against his body. "You're shaking, sweetheart. What's wrong?"

She turned her face and met his gaze. "I'm just happy is all. Scary happy."

"I'm going to make certain you stay that way." He brushed his lips over hers. "Now come on. We don't want to be the last ones on the plane."

"Don't they need you to fly it? What happens after they drop us off in Montana? That was the problem yesterday."

"Already thought of that. It was one of the phone calls I made. One of our agents will meet us at the airport in Missoula. He'll be Roy's copilot for the rest of the trip back to Langley.

You and I will rent a car and drive north to my ranch near Kalispell."

Even though he didn't want to, he let go of Honor and led the way outside and across the base to where the plane waited for them.

"Thank you." Her words were so soft, he thought she might have switched to telepathy.

"No, sweetheart. Thank you. You helped me find a part of myself I thought I'd lost."

"I could say the same thing. I wasn't supposed to have feelings, being a machine and all."

"You were built from human genes," he said, "and don't you ever forget it. See you soon." He pointed to the stairs leading into the plane. "I'll head for the cockpit once we're inside, and you grab a seat in the back."

"I can fly this."

He sent an appraising glance her way. "You can fly the one we rent to come home."

Her eyes lit with delight. "Promise?"

"Promise. Now get moving. The sooner I get this bucket of bolts in the air, the sooner we'll have some private time."

"Your phone will ring."

He snorted. "Not if I don't charge it."

He followed her up the stairs, holding the memory of her warm smile in his heart as he made his way to the left seat in the cockpit. Roy was already there.

"Did you get us preflighted?" Milton asked.

"Yup. We're ready to roll." Roy's blue gaze sharpened. "You're looking like the cat that just ate the canary. What do you have up your sleeve?"

"We're making a slight detour to drop Honor and me in Missoula. We have two days' leave."

"Fantastic!" Roy angled a punch to his ribs. "You're taking her to the ranch, huh?" When Milton nodded, Roy went on. "Maybe that wedding will end up being a double affair."

"You never know, Kincaid. You just never know."

Milton altered their flight plan. That done, he fed new coordinates into the flight computer and received clearance from the tower for takeoff. As the jet taxied and took to the skies, his heart soared right along with it.

~

You've reached the end of *Honor Bound*. This story continues in *Claiming Charity*. Read on for a sample.

ABOUT THE AUTHOR

Ann Gimpel is a USA Today bestselling author. A lifelong aficionado of the unusual, she began writing speculative fiction a few years ago. Since then her short fiction has appeared in a number of webzines, magazines, and anthologies. Her longer books run the gamut from urban fantasy to paranormal romance to science fiction. Once upon a time, she nurtured clients. Now she nurtures dark, gritty fantasy stories that push hard against reality. When she's not writing, she's in the backcountry getting down and dirty with her camera. She's published over 50 books to date, with several more planned for 2018 and beyond. A husband, grown children, grandchildren, and wolf hybrids round out her family.

Keep up with her at www.anngimpel.com or http://anngimpel.blogspot.com

If you enjoyed what you read, get in line for special offers and pre-release special reads. Sign up for Ann's newsletter on her website or her blog.

CLAIMING CHARITY

GENTECH REBELLION, BOOK THREE

harity trudged across Langley's campus, the bare trees a reminder winter had months to go. Night was falling, and a chill damp seeped into her bones, exacerbated by the darkness. It had been damp in the Pacific Northwest where she'd lived before this, but Virginia was a close second.

Hope kept pace with her, seemingly not in a hurry. "You feeling okay?" she asked, keeping her gaze straight ahead.

Charity ground to a halt as irritation flared. "Why does everybody keep asking me that?" She tried for a moderate tone, but sounded like a shrew.

Hope stopped walking too and turned to face her friend. "Because we're genetically modified—in case you'd forgotten. Your genome's unstable because the bastards back at the compound where we lived tried to turn your circuitry from V3 to V4."

"Your point?" Charity gritted out.

Hope trained troubled green eyes on Charity's matching pair. "We were all worried about you. You nearly died."

"You think I'm likely to forget that?" Charity made a fist and punched the air. "Even if I wanted a little distance from something that scared the living shit out of me, none of you will let me forget the slightest detail."

Hope's forehead creased into concerned lines. "Aw, hon—"

Charity made a chopping motion with one hand. "Enough. I'm fine. At least I think I am. That hideous pressure I felt inside me before I collapsed isn't there anymore." She sucked in air, seeking a place beyond anger. "We're both tired. That last mission was a bitch."

"We need to let Faith know we're back." Hope started walking toward the building that housed their apartments.

After a pause, Charity caught up with her. "Yeah, she probably worried about us while we were gone. Her legs should be healed up by now, so she'll want to be at the meeting tomorrow at zero seven hundred."

"How'd you find out about it?" Hope angled to face her, but kept moving. "No one told me. I figured we'd hold off on anything for a couple days—until Milton and Honor get back from that ranch of his in Montana."

The corners of Charity's mouth twitched into half a grin. "Did you see the looks on their faces before they got out of the plane in Missoula?"

Hope snorted. "Did I ever? Like the second they got out of our sight, he was going to back her up against a building, rip her pants off, and screw her senseless."

"I hope they're as happy as Roy and Glory," Charity murmured. "After what we lived through, we all deserve hot dudes who worship the ground we walk on."

"No kidding, huh?" Hope tipped her head to engage the retinal scanner outside their building. After a moment, the door clicked open. She nodded at the ever-present lobby guard and motioned Charity toward the stairwell. "How'd you find out about the meeting?" she persisted. "You never did tell me."

Heat traveled from her chest upward, and Charity chided herself for a much-too-human reaction to Tony, one of the genetically altered men who'd defected to help the CIA. "From Tony. Guess Charlie told him to pass it down the line."

"Sheesh. Charlie's our team leader. You'd think he could tell us himself."

"He and Roy were called into a meeting with the brass. I suppose they got tapped because Milton isn't here." Charity trotted into the stairwell behind Hope. None of them liked elevators. They'd come from a life where they trained six to eight hours a day. By contrast, life at the CIA compound was soft and cushy.

When Charity walked through the door at the top of the stairwell, Faith raced toward them, a huge grin on her face. Before Charity could say a word, Faith hugged them both soundly murmuring, "I'm damned glad you're back. When I felt your energy, I couldn't just wait in my apartment. Had to lay eyes on you."

"Oh ye of little faith." Charity made a pun. "Did you think we were so puny we couldn't get through a raid on the Nameless Ones' headquarters?"

Faith let go, so excited she bounced up and down. Like all of them, she was six feet tall, with waist length black hair, and cat green eyes. Today, she wore gray sweats emblazoned with the CIA logo. "Tell me what happened. Everything. I was afraid you'd skip bothering me until morning, and by then curiosity would've swallowed me whole." She swept an appraising glance over them. "You probably want to clean up. I'll tag along, and you can fill me in."

"Good plan." Charity nodded, feeling wiped out. "Feel free to link up with me, and then Hope can join us after her shower."

Faith pushed the stairwell door open and stared down it before turning to face the other women. Her smile faded, replaced by a pinched look. "Where's Honor? I know Glory's with Roy, but—"

"In Montana with Milton at a cattle ranch." Hope waggled her eyebrows suggestively.

Faith exhaled briskly and broke into laughter. "Awesome! I wish them every happiness. Come on. Let's get moving, so you can tell me everything. I want all the dirty details."

Charity covered the fifty feet to her door and tilted her chin so the retinal scanner would let her into her apartment. Faith stuck to her like a shadow.

"See you soon." Hope's voice echoed as she moved farther down the hall to her quarters.

"How are the legs?" Charity asked and sat to unlace her muddy boots, which she then toed off, followed by her socks.

"Healed. I'm back at a hundred percent." Faith beamed. "I was good to go about twenty-four hours after you left, but by then it was too late." She made a face. "Like the CIA would've sent a special plane with just me in it. What the hell happened? It was like a funeral home around her for those few hours when everyone was certain Milton was dead."

"Wasn't real cheery where we were, either." Charity stood and unzipped her field jacket, hanging it on a hook. She systematically stripped off the rest of her clothes, all of which went into the laundry hamper. "Basically, the Nameless Ones booby-trapped the underground escape passageway leading to the subterranean computer room. Milton made it to the room before the explosion, but he couldn't let any of us know because the chamber's shielded with metal. Follow me if you want to hear more."

Charity trudged into the small bathroom, turned on the shower, and got under its spray. So she wouldn't have to shout, she switched to telepathy. *"Anyway, I guess Milton tried to merge with the computer— like we do—decided he didn't know enough to go that route, and so he stole the hard drives instead."*

"How'd he get out if the passageways were blown to bits?"

"I'm a little hazy on that, but I guess there was another passageway he discovered by accident."

"Thank God for that. We need him."

Charity thought about that as she sluiced shampoo from her hair. She'd lived in a dorm with eleven other women at a special hidden compound for seven years. Hundreds of similar compounds were located throughout the world. Her memory of her life before the compound was nonexistent, as if someone erased that part of her central processing unit. She turned off the water and drew the curtain back.

Faith handed her a towel. "You're pretty quiet."

"I was thinking about what you said. The part about needing Milton." She blotted water from her body and wound the towel around her head. "I understand he's the head of the CIA, and single-handedly responsible for deciding we were worth rescuing, but for years the only ones we needed were us."

"When it got down to it," Faith shot a pointed glance her way, "seven of us, didn't trust Glory enough to go with her the night she offered us a chance at freedom."

Charity winced. Those seven women were dead, a point that still made her heart hurt. The twelve of them had been like sisters, united against the men—Nameless Ones—and their ironclad control over all the women. Even simple things like food, heat, and clothing were rationed.

She knew now the genetically altered men rode herd on them because the women's design was so far superior, but she didn't know it then. The Nameless Ones' strict rules rankled, until all the women wanted nothing more than to wipe out every last one of them.

Glory had killed one of the men—to sidestep being raped. It was why she ran away: to avoid living out the rest of her life in an iso cell… But if she hadn't run, she'd never have met Roy, and Charity and the rest of them would still be stuck in their compound, functioning as one step up from slaves.

Charity made her way past Faith. She rustled clean navy blue sweats from a drawer and pulled them on over her still-damp body. A sharp tap at the door announced Hope on the other side. Charity sent a mental blast of energy to twist the locking mechanism.

"Hiya!" Hope's hair hung down her back in damp curls. She hugged Faith. "All caught up, hon?"

"Pretty much. Any idea what comes next?"

"Not really. Are either of you hungry?"

"Me!" Charity snugged her feet into a pair of running shoes.

"I'll keep you company if you're headed for the cafeteria," Faith said. She patted her hips. "Probably don't need another meal, but I can have a cup of coffee."

Charity glanced at her. "You don't look heavier."

"I'm probably not, but I couldn't get much exercise while my broken legs healed, and the only thing left to do was eat." She shrugged. "Let's get some food into the two of you. Bet you'd love to have an uninterrupted night's sleep."

"Last night wasn't so bad," Charity cut in. "We were in the Air Force barracks in Colorado Springs. At least Hope and I were. Glory was with Roy, and Honor was with Milton."

"Yeah, you already mentioned that." Faith smirked. "Sounds like someone's wishing for a guy all for herself."

"Shut up." Charity mock slugged her before grabbing a coat and leading the way out of her apartment. She'd spent the last seven years hating the Nameless Ones. Hell would freeze over before she paid even the slightest heed to Tony's interest in her. He probably just wanted to get laid, but she was less than interested.

He saved my life.

So what? It doesn't mean I owe him shit.

TONY DIALED his night vision up another notch and paced Frank as they ran hard around Langley's perimeter. After being cooped up for hours in a plane, both men needed to burn off some steam. As Tony ran, scenes from his computer-like brain flashed before him.

After his petri dish birth on one of the breeding farms set up by the U.S. government, he'd been groomed from adolescence to work as a genetic researcher. None of them attended school; their knowledge was downloaded directly from huge mainframes operated by government scientists. He lived a comfortable life at his breeding farm near Portland, Oregon, but it blew up in his face seven years ago. He was twenty-two then and knee-deep in research to perfect those like him. Each successive strain was a bit better than the last, but problems still cropped up.

He'd been close to a major breakthrough—at least he thought he was, but it could've been a dead end like so much of his research—when a cadre of renegade freaks, genetically engineered humans just like him, staged a rebellion. They hadn't cared for the decision to scrap the earlier prototypes, so they blew up every breeding farm they could find. After that, they created hidden compounds, like the one in Keyser, West Virginia where Tony ended up.

He hadn't bought into the violence, but there wasn't a hell of a lot of choice once it began. Normal humans shot them on sight after the rebellion, so he went along with the program and moved his genetic research to his assigned compound. He didn't have nearly the access to materials he'd had prior to the rebellion, but at least he was still alive.

"You're pretty quiet, buddy," Frank observed.

"Sorry. I was thinking."

The other man snorted. "Always dangerous. About what? Did you come up with something we missed on those hard drives Milton swiped from our headquarters?"

"Nah. Wish it were that straightforward."

Frank slugged him in the arm. "Watch that esoteric stuff. Our programming's not designed for it."

"Maybe not, but do you ever wonder what will become of us?"

"The probability of that line of thought producing something of value is—"

"Not what I asked," Tony snapped. "We've thrown in our lot with normal humans, V0 as it were. We can't undo it."

"So? You and I discussed this before we showed ourselves and requested amnesty. We could've remained hidden. They would have found Charity without our help, and then they'd have left. We didn't take that route. Are you having second thoughts?"

"Not really. We didn't fit in with the other Nameless Ones—except it was a ridiculous moniker, since we had names, we just didn't tell them to the women." Tony slowed when they came to a perimeter fence and turned to face the other man. Because of the physical strength built into his genetics, he wasn't even slightly winded.

Frank stopped and tossed his hood back. Shaggy black hair fell to his shoulders, and he examined Tony through his amber, animal-like eyes with vertical slit pupils. All the men looked very much the same due to shared genetics. Tall, rangy, muscled. Both of them wore regulation issue CIA field gear they hadn't changed out of yet.

"What aren't you saying?" Frank asked.

"Not sure. Except I'm feeling like a man without a country. We didn't fit in there, but we don't fit in here, either. They don't trust us. I saw it in Milton's eyes that night you and I saved Charity's life."

Frank grimaced. "Shit, bro. We're machines. We're not supposed to have feelings. Who cares if they trust us, so long as they continue to offer us a place to work and live? When did you fall off the wagon?"

Should I?

Tony weighed the advisability of confiding in Frank, but if not him, then whom?

"Talk, or I'm going back to my apartment. I'm fine when we're moving, but I'm getting cold. Can't be much more than fifteen degrees out here. In fact," Frank sent a short blurt of power outward, "it's eighteen point three Fahrenheit, but there's a five knot wind, which brings the ambient temperature to—"

"Never mind that. I know it's cold without a weather report. I have a problem that runs deeper than the humans not trusting us. They made a commitment to us, same as we did to them. The odds of them welching on the deal—so long as we don't fuck them over—is under twelve percent."

Frank furled his brows. "Okay. So you have a problem. Is it something we could hash out inside where it's warm?"

"I think better when I'm cold."

"Fine." Frank gestured with a gloved hand. "Whatever it is, get it out, so we can chase down something to eat and find our beds."

Tony unclenched his jaw. It was either spit it out or shut up. Running probabilities about Frank's reaction wouldn't alter his choices. He squared his shoulders and began to talk. "I spent a long time—hours—linked to Charity when she was so compromised. I was the one who sent my energy into her."

"I haven't forgotten. So?"

"I developed a fondness for her during that time." Very unmachine-like feelings tightened Tony's gut.

Frank's eyes widened. "Oh ho! You want to fuck her. I'm not seeing where that's a problem. The women were off limits to us at the compounds, but the CIA doesn't have those kind of rules."

The unmachine-like feelings intensified, and Tony felt his face grow warm. "Yeah, I want her that way, but it's more than that. I like her. She's a bitch, sure, but she's fresh and funny and spunky. We drummed the spirit out of so many of the women, but not her."

"Have you talked with her about any of this?"

Tony shook his head. "No."

"Why not? Seems to me that'd be the logical place to start."

A snort blew past Tony's lips. "Yeah, huh? Problem is I got a pretty good look inside her head. She hates us."

Frank drew back. "Why? She never even met us before she and her group attacked our compound."

Tony shook his head again. "It runs deeper than that. She hates all of us men—for how we treated her and the other women. Even if that weren't there, it must've been appalling for her when she discovered the V4s slaughtered the females in our compound. Her team planned to rescue them. The V4s figured it out and beat them to the punch."

"Yeah, but none of that was personal—" Frank began.

"Try telling her that. I'm sure it felt goddamned personal. Christ!

The women's bodies weren't even cold when Charity stumbled onto them."

"I'm not sure Charity found them, but the women who did certainly told her about it." Frank jerked his chin in the general direction of their apartment building. "Let's get moving." When Tony fell into step with him, he went on. "Seems to me you've really only got two choices. One. You suck it up and keep quiet. We weren't exactly designed to have mates. All our babies were created in test tubes—even after the breeding farms."

"That was because we were afraid the women would pick our brains during sex, discover how powerful they were, and demand equality."

"It doesn't matter why," Frank replied. "Even though I was a minority, I never believed it would've been the end of the world if the women discovered their innate power, but they didn't. Over time, we got away from intercourse as a primary source of procreation."

"We're getting off course. What's my second option?"

"Sit down and talk to her. Tell her how you feel."

Tony rolled the probabilities of how that would go through his brain. "Less than an eighteen percent chance she'd be open to it," he muttered.

Frank didn't respond, and they ran the rest of the way to their building in silence. Once they were inside, Tony said, "Thanks."

"For what? I didn't help much. See you tomorrow at zero seven hundred." Frank turned down the hallway that led to his apartment.

Tony climbed a flight of stairs to his quarters and let himself in. If getting something going with Charity was such a crapshoot, why couldn't he let go of the idea?

When the answer came, he didn't like it much. He'd broken protocol to save her, blending his energy with hers in an intimate pattern that wasn't in any of the manuals. Apparently she'd gotten under his skin during the process, and now he was stuck. When he wasn't busy, she was all he thought about.

He stripped out of his heavy field coat and tossed it over a chair. The rest of his clothes ended up in a heap on the floor. Everything could stand a tour through the washing machine, but not tonight. He headed for the bathroom and a shower with his cock standing out like a ship's prow. He was hard almost all the time now, despite jacking off two or three times a day. Hard because he wanted her.

Crap!

He pulled the shower curtain aside. Once he got the water going, he stepped over the high rim of the tub. Even though he tried not to, his hands found their way to his engorged flesh, and somewhere between the soap and hot water, he made himself come with visions of what he thought Charity's perfect, naked body would look like plastered behind his eyes.